RIVER *of* FIRE

Nancy Gentry

To Anne, my friend and inspiration.

Experience the last voyage of the Sultana.

Nancy Gentry

NG Books

Copyright © 2015 by Nancy Gentry

All rights reserved. This book or any portion thereof may not be reproduced or used in any manner whatsoever without the express written permission of the publisher except for the use of brief quotations in a book review.

Printed in the United States of America

Written by Nancy Gentry
Edited by Jessa Sexton
Graphic Design by Mike Bullard
Interior illustrations by Casey Smith

First Printing, 2015
Version 1.0
ISBN 978-0-692-54136-4

NG Books
Memphis, TN

www.RebelinPetticoats.com

DEDICATION

This book is dedicated to the victims and survivors of the *Sultana*. It is their story, and one that should not be forgotten.

In memory of my dad, Jim Henry Burks.

ACKNOWLEDGEMENTS

Having such a talented, creative, and enthusiastic team to turn my story into this wonderful book is truly a blessing for which I am extremely grateful. My deepest gratitude goes to Jessa Sexton who has been on this journey with me from the beginning. She has touched each of my books with her expertise, professionalism, and love of writing. I appreciate her gift for writing, her keen sense for editing, and her special friendship.

Many thanks go to Mike Bullard for the many hours and hard work he devoted to designing *River of Fire*. His enthusiasm for this project was matched only by his passion for doing the best job possible. He shares my belief that this story needs to be passed along to young readers, and his personal interest was so encouraging to me. I appreciate his vision for the book, his expertise in book design, and his devotion to his work.

Beautiful illustrations help young readers better visualize a story, and for these I would like to thank Casey Smith. He is an extremely talented artist who embraced this project with enthusiasm and vision. Being an elementary art teacher, Casey understands a child's perspective which made him a perfect fit for illustrating this story. I appreciate his artistic talent, his interpretation of the story through pictures, and his dedication to this story.

As always, my sincere thanks go to my family and friends who not only continue to support me, but who stay excited about my projects and encourage me. Sharing my writing and my books with others brings such joy.

PREFACE

One hundred and fifty years have passed since the magnificent riverboat *Sultana* made her last voyage on the mighty Mississippi River. On April 27, 1865 around 2:00 a.m. with an estimated 2300 passengers on board, and possibly as many as 2500, her boilers exploded. The death toll has never been pinpointed with an exact number, but estimates say as many as 1800 passengers died in the fire or in the chilly waters of the river. Out of these casualties, only 167 were civilians and crew. Ironically, the rest were Union ex-prisoners of war finally on their way home after surviving the long, cruel Civil War.

The explosion of the *Sultana* has been described as the worst maritime disaster in U.S history, and possibly even in world history as the number of fatalities exceeds even that of the famous *Titanic*. Yet, few people today recognize the name *Sultana*. Why has this great human tragedy never received the attention the many lost lives deserve?

At the time of the disaster our nation was still reeling from four terrible years of the war. People were weary from the long casualty lists of devastating battles that, in the end, totaled over 600,000 men. Nearly every family north and south had suffered losses of loved ones. The nation was mourning the recent death of President Abraham Lincoln whose body was making its way across the country when the *Sultana* exploded. The tragedy on the Mississippi was yet another reminder of the curtain of death that shrouded our nation, and to put it aside, so as not to have to think on it, seemed to be the course of action at the time. Time has not revived the recognition of the great riverboat and its lost passengers.

River of Fire is a story about the *Sultana's* final journey up the Mississippi. Although this book is historical fiction, the fictional characters parallel real-life passengers, and the events are historically accurate. I use a fictional frame to bring the passengers to life and connect you, the reader, to the real people of this disaster. This is their story, a story that should be passed down through the generations and forever kept alive.

Meet Elizabeth
April 23, 1865

Standing on the upper deck of the giant riverboat, Elizabeth took in a deep breath and smiled. The cool, spring wind felt good on her face. It felt like freedom. No, it *was* freedom. After four long years, the terrible War Between the States was over. Her family was leaving their home in Louisiana and heading north to build a new life. Elizabeth was sure the man she would marry was waiting for her there. This was her dream, and her whole life lay ahead of her. What a great adventure it was going to be!

Leaning out over the deck rail, Elizabeth watched the huge boat break the current as it pushed upstream. Large logs, tree branches, and other debris swirled past in small eddies as they flowed downstream. The Mississippi was at flood stage, stretching almost four miles from eastern to western banks. Though it was a treacherous river, for sure, right now it felt like a magic carpet to a new world for Elizabeth.

Just as she leaned farther over the rail, stretching her arms out as if to fly, a hand clasped on her wrist and jerked her back.

"Stop it!" the voice yelled. "Elizabeth, why do you have to be so daring?"

Elizabeth stumbled backwards but caught herself before she fell. She turned to see her older brother Dee.

"Dee, please," Elizabeth caught her breath. "Don't be silly. This is not daring."

Still holding her wrist, Dee shook his head and looked at her angrily.

"One jolt from this boat could have sent you over the rail and into that icy, cold water." He flung his free arm out toward the water to emphasize his point.

They both looked at the swift current and rolling waves.

"How do you think that would feel?" he spit the words at her. "You can't swim, remember?"

Elizabeth pulled free from his grip and smiled.

"You distress yourself too much over me, my dear brother." She gently touched his cheek. He was nineteen, only two years older than she, but he often treated her like a little child.

"I am a young woman and will watch out for myself," she said, still smiling.

"You, my dear sister, are a young *girl,* and you should act like one." Dee was still frowning as he spoke.

For a brief moment Elizabeth studied her brother's face. Even with this ridiculous scowl, he was a handsome fellow. His olive complexion, dark wavy hair, and deep brown eyes had captured many young girls' hearts . . . and broken them when he said goodbye. Strangers sometimes asked if they were twins, but even though they had similar skin tones and hair, Elizabeth's eyes were dark blue, and she never considered herself to be beautiful.

As Elizabeth watched her brother his face gradually began to soften. Whether it was the sparkle in her eyes, the fresh wind blowing on his face, or feeling the same sense of freedom that had grabbed Elizabeth, he was soon smiling, too. Looking out over the muddy, churning water, he took a deep breath. Both brother and sister were caught up in all the possibilities of the new home and bright future; neither one of them wanted to break the spell of this moment.

But, shaking himself back to reality, Dee turned to Elizabeth and said, "Mother sent me to get you. We dock in Vicksburg in a few hours, and she wants you to freshen up."

Elizabeth sighed. She felt fresh enough, but Mother always wanted her to do more.

"She also needs help with Catherine."

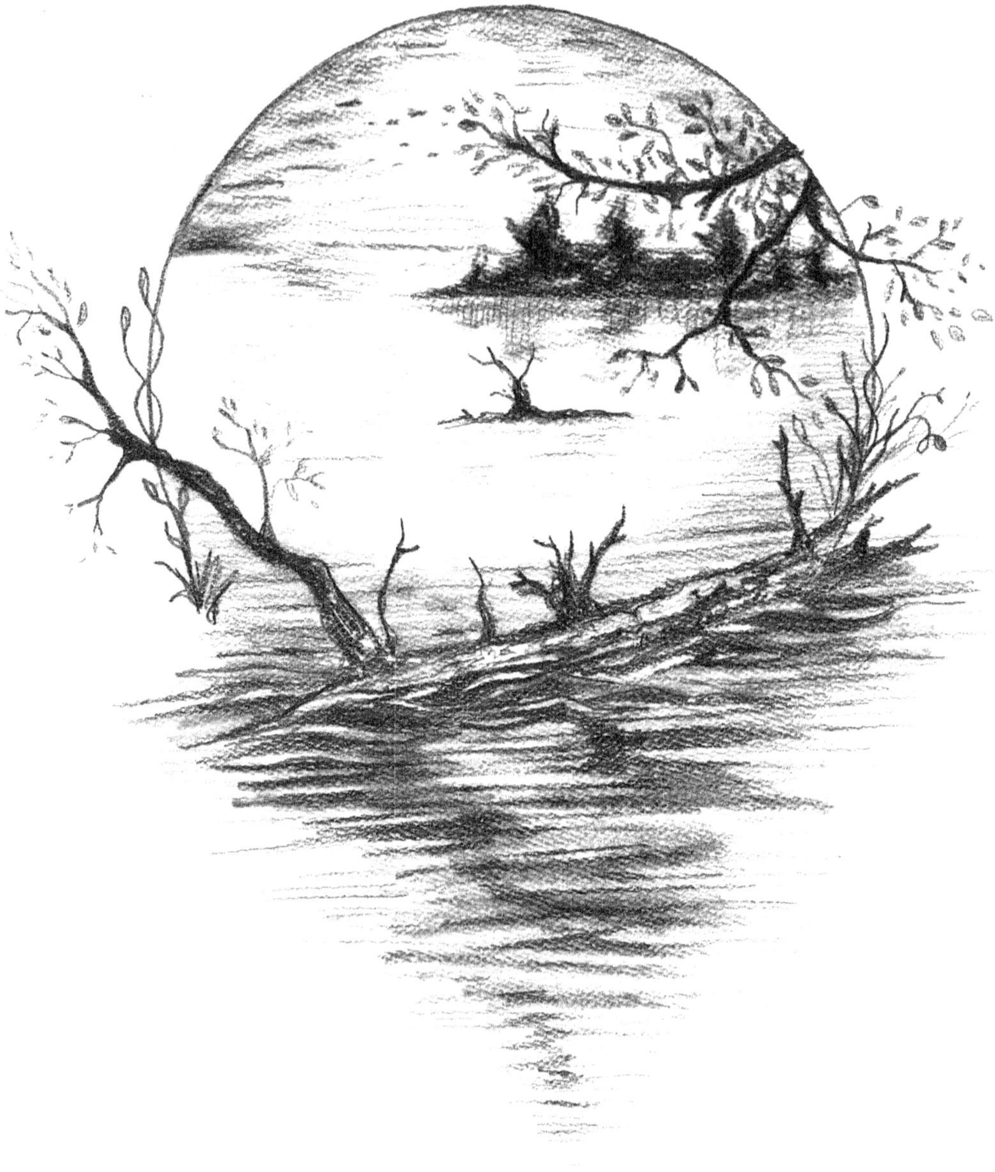

"Oh, all right," Elizabeth said with a deeper sigh. She knew her mother was not in the best health and did not have the strength to take care of a six-year-old child's needs. Her little sister Catherine came along ten years after her parents thought their family was complete. Catherine's birth was especially difficult for their mother who never recovered her former health. The past few difficult years during the war had only worsened Mother's condition. So Elizabeth took over the care of the little girl who was more like her own child than her sister. She loved that little girl more than anything else in the world.

Lingering a few minutes more, Elizabeth watched the sun's rays glinting off the water as it dropped lower in the sky. They had been on the steamboat two days, two glorious days. Each stop had been a new adventure, and now they were almost to Vicksburg, Mississippi, as far north as Elizabeth had ever been in her life. She knew it would not be the same Vicksburg she remembered from her childhood visits. The war had almost crushed the life out of the busy city. Under siege and shelling from Grant's army, the people of Vicksburg had fled or been forced to dig caves in which to live for safety. Their homes had been destroyed, and their lives shattered. Elizabeth did not want to see the destruction and reminders of the hardships endured there, but it was one necessary step closer to her dreams.

Heading for the stairs that led to the middle deck where the cabins were, Dee spoke again, "And one more thing. After we dock at Vicksburg, Father says you must stay in the cabin for the remainder of the journey, no more roaming around the boat."

"What?" Elizabeth exclaimed in disbelief. There were few passengers on the steamboat, and she had been allowed to explore every inch of the boat as she pleased. Being confined to the cabin would drive her absolutely mad.

"Father has been told that in Vicksburg there will be many Union soldiers, former prisoners of war, joining us," Dee continued. "They're being shipped home, and Father does not want you in the midst of them."

"Oh, this is ridiculous," Elizabeth huffed. "How can a few soldiers be of any danger to me?"

She looked back at Dee who simply looked tired, tired of being the messenger and the one who had to argue with Elizabeth.

Elizabeth stomped away from her brother, feeling defeated. She could usually sway Dee into doing anything she wanted, but she knew she could not win an argument against her father. The wonderful bubble she had just been floating on suddenly burst, and her mood soured.

As she entered the cabin the room was surprisingly quiet. Was Catherine asleep? Then, suddenly out of nowhere, Elizabeth was grabbed from behind, and nearly knocked off her feet.

"Boo!" shouted a little voice. "Bethie, where have you been? I've had no one to play with for hours."

Swinging around and scooping up the little girl, Elizabeth tumbled on the floor and rolled around, both of them giggling and squealing.

"What's all this?" they heard their mother say from the bedroom. She appeared at the door, shaking her head and holding onto the back of a chair. "Why must you girls play so rough? You act more like wild bucks than young ladies."

"Sorry, Mother," Elizabeth said as she picked up herself and Catherine, smoothing both their dresses and hair. "We were just having a little fun." Elizabeth winked at Catherine who covered her mouth and giggled again.

"Please, Elizabeth, help your sister with her hair and make sure you're both ready for supper," Mother turned to lie down again but stopped and added, "Your father says you are to stay in the cabin when we dock at Vicksburg. No going out to watch the new passengers board."

Elizabeth sighed but simply said, "Yes, ma'am."

It was dark by the time the steamboat finally tied up at the Vicksburg landing. There was little activity at this time, and Elizabeth remained confused over her father's concerns about the anticipated passengers and continued to fume over the restrictions placed on her.

At supper Father was especially harsh, not letting Elizabeth speak, or rather, argue about it. His stern gaze was like a clamp on her mouth as he insisted that both his daughters be limited to the cabin and hallway. This not only hurt Elizabeth's feelings but also made her feel like a little child.

Later, Dee pulled her aside to explain Father's attitude.

"Elizabeth, you must not push Father about his decision," Dee whispered between his teeth so their parents wouldn't hear. "Mother got very upset when she found out the prisoners were boarding the *Sultana*. Father went so far as to try to get a refund, so he could book passage for the family on another steamboat."

Elizabeth's eyes were wide with surprise to hear this.

"Captain Mason refused to return Father's money, so we're stuck on this boat." Dee squeezed Elizabeth's elbow to make his point. "Mother is still upset, so just obey Father and say no more."

Elizabeth understood but was still confused. How could a few Union soldiers be a threat to her? They were no longer the enemy but simply passengers. But because their presence brought on her confinement, Elizabeth's resentment toward these men rose to the boiling point. She could not allow these intruders to spoil her freedom.

Later, as Elizabeth lay in the dark trying to go to sleep, she was still pondering the situation. Being pent up in the cabin would be unbearable, and she was sure there was an answer to all this. She just needed a plan. Tomorrow would be a new day, bringing with it, a new hope. She was sure she would think of something. And with that optimistic thought, she drifted off to sleep.

Vicksburg

April 24, 1865

As the sun rose over Vicksburg the next morning, Elizabeth was awakened by a sudden ray of light coming through a small, shuttered window of the sitting room where she slept. Running the back of her hand across her face, she tried to open her eyes.

"Are you awake, Bethie?" a small voice called.

Of course, it was her little sister. As punctual as a rooster at dawn, she would wake her "Bethie" each morning and act surprised when Elizabeth opened her eyes. Catherine couldn't stand for her older sister to sleep when she was up.

"Well, I am *now*," Elizabeth managed to clear her throat to speak. "But, oh, I was having the most beautiful dream."

"Tell me, Bethie, tell me about your dream." The little girl jumped and landed on the edge of the sofa where her older sister lay.

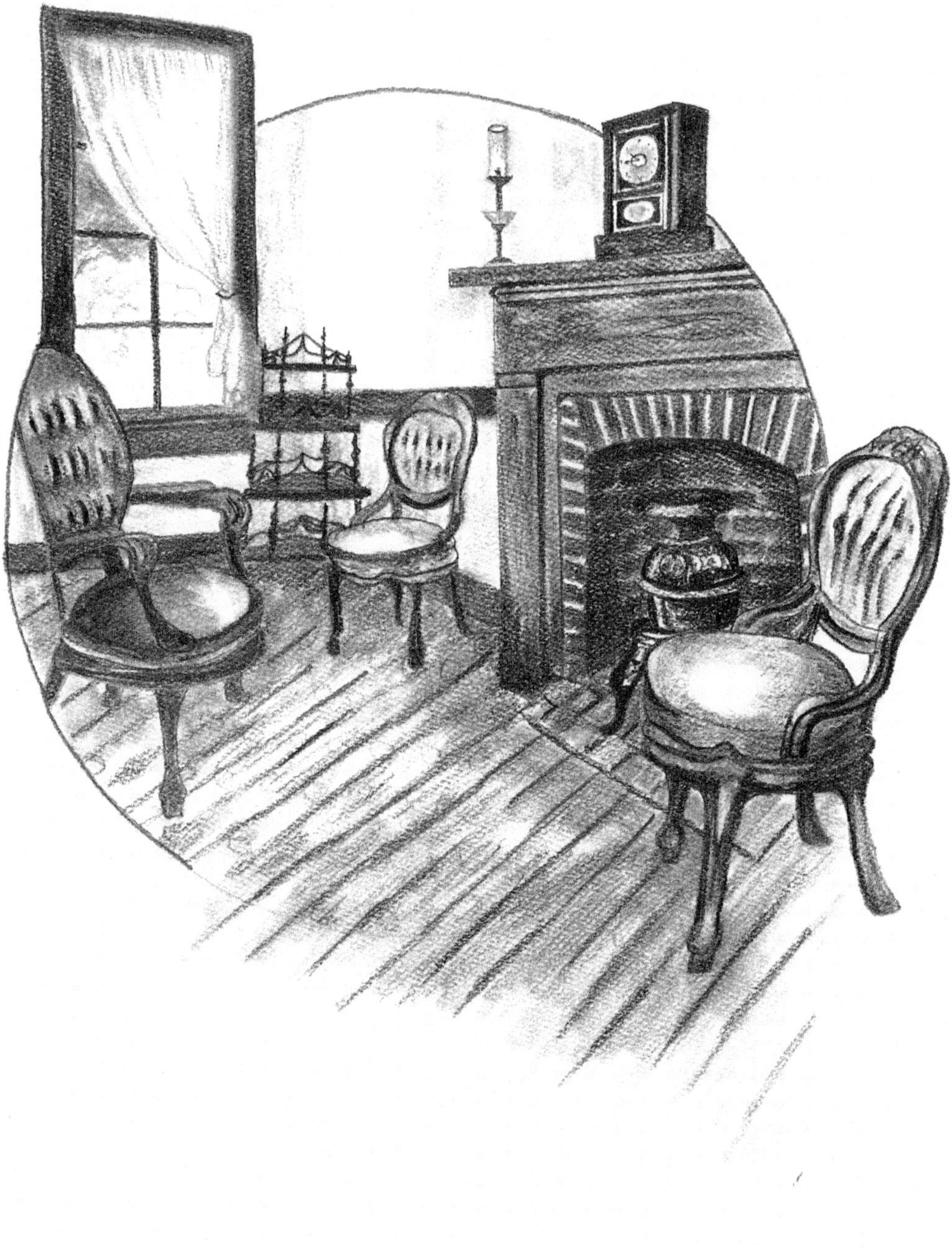

"Oh, Catherine, there was a ballroom, a big grand ballroom," Elizabeth began as she closed her eyes as if to see it all again. "There was a sea of ball gowns, hoop skirts like giant bells, swirling around to the most beautiful music. Everything was gold and glittery."

Listening with big, round eyes, Catherine clasped her sister's hand in her smaller ones.

"Then suddenly, I was swept off my feet by a pair of big strong arms," Elizabeth's voice rose with excitement. "And off to the dance floor we flew."

"Who was it , Bethie?" the little girl asked excitedly. "Who swept you off your feet?"

Fully awake now, Elizabeth opened her eyes and looked straight at her sister.

"I don't know," Elizabeth sprang up and grabbed Catherine around the waist. "You woke me up before I could find out."

Then she tickled Catherine until the child squealed, and they both fell off the sofa.

"Girls, girls, please," they heard their mother say from the bed in the next room. The cabin was so small that it was impossible not to hear every small noise, much less a very loud one.

"Sorry, mother," both girls said together.

Catherine whispered in her sister's ear, "Mother's not feeling well today. She's got another one of her headaches."

Elizabeth nodded with understanding and began standing up when she heard a soft tap on the door. It was Father and Dee bringing hot tea and cakes for their breakfast. The men of the family had secured a different cabin next to them to have enough places for everyone to sleep.

The small sitting room seemed even smaller when Father stepped in, ducking slightly to clear the low door. As usual, Father was dressed neatly in a long, black coat, white shirt, and tie. His black mustache and beard were trimmed closely to his face. Father was a handsome man, Elizabeth thought, if only he would smile more.

Setting down the tray on a small table, Father bent down to sweep up Catherine who jumped into his arms. Catherine was the light of their father's life, and she simply adored him.

After a big bear hug Father set down his little girl, straightened up, and turned to Elizabeth.

"Good morning, dear," Father said. "Did you sleep well?"

He gestured to the sofa on which she had spent the night. Mother and Catherine had taken the one bed, and she had no choice but to make the best of this sleeping arrangement.

"Yes, I slept fine," Elizabeth smiled at Father as he stroked her hair with affection. Although Father and Elizabeth often disagreed and her constant struggle for independence exhausted him, Father admired his daughter's spirit. It was the same spirit that had attracted him to his wife, a spirit that had slowly slipped away with the years and the children. He only wished he knew how to better handle the constant problems his daughter created.

"Now, Elizabeth," Father locked his own blue eyes on hers and spoke in his most serious tone. Elizabeth braced herself for the instructions she knew were coming.

"Remember our talk last night. You must stay in the cabin from now on," Father paused for her reaction.

"But, Father..." Elizabeth protested.

"Now, now, listen to me," Father stood his ground. "There will be many soldiers boarding soon. Many are sick and dirty, and you need to stay out of their way."

The frown of disappointment on Elizabeth's face tugged at Father's heart. It felt like he was caging a beautiful bird, but he had no choice. He gently held both of her shoulders so Elizabeth was forced to face him.

"Dee and I are going into town to see an old friend and check on things of business," Father squeezed her arms to make his point. "You must promise me you'll stay in while we're gone."

"But, Father," Elizabeth continued to protest. "Can't I go with you? Please?"

Father shook his head and lowered his eyes from her

pleading ones.

"No," he replied with a sigh. "It's no place for a young woman. Besides, you're needed here to watch after your mother and Catherine."

Elizabeth wanted to stomp her foot in protest. She hated being the young woman who always had to stay in her *place*. But she also knew her father was right, and she understood how much Father needed her here.

As Father turned to leave, Elizabeth stole a glance at Dee who was watching her with pleading eyes of his own. By the look on his face, she knew he was begging her to obey their father. Dee grew tired of the constant turmoil Elizabeth stirred up with her strong will. Secretly, he envied her courage and high spirits, a trait he had not acquired to any degree. Dee was still wrestling with the fact that he had not gone to war.

Actually, he had wanted to enlist when the war began, at age fifteen, but Father had forbidden him to do so until he was eighteen. By that time the war was going badly for the South, and it seemed useless to join a defeated army. Many of his friends had fought, some never returning, others coming home with missing arms or legs. Even so, Dee wished he had gone. Staying home and helping Father sustain the family despite a failing business could not equal being a soldier, and Dee feared he would never redeem himself.

With the men gone, Elizabeth and Catherine settled down to a quiet breakfast. Not wanting to disturb their sleeping mother who refused to join them, they did not speak. More than that, Elizabeth was straining to hear the sounds outside the cabin. Failing to notice any unusual voices or commotion, she went to the window and peered out the narrow slats of the shutter.

"What is it, Bethie?" Catherine whispered. "Have the soldiers come aboard yet?"

"No," replied Elizabeth. "Not a soul has boarded that I can tell, and we have a perfect view of the boarding plank."

The wheels in Elizabeth's brain began to spin. Biting her lip, she studied her little sister who was watching her with wide eyes.

"What is it, Bethie?" she asked again in a whisper. "What are you going to do?" The little girl's face clearly revealed her worry.

Moving away from the window and bending down to Catherine's eye level, Elizabeth look squarely at her sister.

"You can't disobey Father, Bethie," she raised her voice a little too high, and Elizabeth put her finger to Catherine's lips to hush her.

"I don't plan to disobey Father," replied Elizabeth. "Actually, he said *when* the soldiers board to stay out of their way. Well, they're not here yet."

"Please, Bethie, don't leave me here with Mother," the little girl begged. "Please don't go."

In a flash Elizabeth's mind planned it all out. She would take Catherine with her as a partner-in-crime. That way, even in her greatest excitement, the child would not let it slip to Father or Dee.

"Oh, no, Catherine," Elizabeth reassured her. "You'll come with me. Let's take a short, very short, stroll around the deck. We don't want to leave Mother long, and if the soldiers come, we'll dash back to the cabin."

The child's face lit up, and she started to clap in excitement. Grabbing Catherine's hands in her own, Elizabeth reminded her to be quiet by giving a nod toward their sleeping mother. Then they both began getting dressed. Elizabeth brushed Catherine's light brown hair that was so different from the rest of the family's dark, almost black, hair. Besides having the same blue eyes, the two sisters did not look much alike, Catherine being fair in complexion and Elizabeth having her brother's olive-tone skin.

Once Elizabeth pulled up her own long black hair into a net that lay neatly on her neck, she quietly opened the cabin door, and the two girls slipped out into the hallway. Making their way to the door that opened onto the deck, they were surprised by a shrill voice and noisy laughter behind them. Both girls spun around to see what was happening.

At the other end of the long hallway that ran between the cabins, a door had opened, and two women dressed in gaudy colors stepped out. One wore a bright red dress, a big plume in her hat, and a red boa wrapped around her neck. The other was dressed in purple with an equally large feather sticking up from her over-sized hat. Two men followed them, one dressed in a ridiculous plaid suit and the other in a dark red jacket and pants. Elizabeth had seen them before and knew they were part of a performing troupe that was headed to Memphis. Her mother would be horrified to think her daughters were in the company of such people. Elizabeth quickly turned Catherine back around and pushed her through the outer door to shield her from seeing. Four loud voices and laughter were still audible through the closed door.

Nearly blinded by the bright sunlight, both girls shielded their eyes and waited until they could focus once again. Walking to the railing of the deck, they both breathed in the fresh air and smiled. They looked down at the muddy water that splashed against the docked riverboat.

"Oh, Bethie," Catherine was still whispering. "It's so beautiful!"

"Well, I don't know about beautiful," Elizabeth said. "But it is a sight to see."

It wasn't just the river that was fascinating, but all the activity that was taking place on the landing. As they watched, men were everywhere, yelling orders, moving here and there, pulling ropes, and loading boxes, barrels, and horses. What a beehive of human activity it was, and Elizabeth was thrilled to be a witness.

Somewhere in the midst of all the noise, Elizabeth could hear a steady clanging sound, a sound that she hadn't heard before on the boat.

"Come on," Elizabeth took her sister's hand and headed for the stairs that led to the main deck.

"Where are we going?" Catherine asked. "I thought we were just going out on the deck for a few minutes."

"You hear that sound?" Elizabeth was trying to distract her sister as she led her down the stairs. "Let's go see what it is."

It was not so much her curiosity that drew Elizabeth to the sound but her need to move about. They walked as quickly as they could on the crowded deck until they reached the giant wheelhouse. Then Catherine stopped abruptly to look at the large paddlewheel. It fascinated her, and she stared in awe. Tugging on her little sister's hand to move her along, Elizabeth urged, "We don't have much time."

On the main level of the boat the deck was busier and noisier. Nearing the boiler room, the two girls dodged sweaty men covered in black soot from head to toe. There was yelling, grunting, and the clanging sound was louder than ever.

Just as Elizabeth was about to peer into the door, someone shouted gruffly, "Stop there, ladies."

Whirling around in the direction of the voice, Elizabeth saw a stout, bearded man with a huge cigar hanging from his mouth. He was dressed in dirty, baggy pants and a loose, grimy shirt. His hair was greasy and hung in tangled strands, and the few teeth he had were an ugly, yellowish brown. Instinctively, Elizabeth pulled Catherine around behind her back to shield the little girl from the man's glare.

"What are you doing here?" the man grunted as his cigar bobbed up and down between his lips.

"Sir, we just want to see what that sound is," Elizabeth explained nervously. "We didn't mean to cause any trouble."

Removing his cigar and pointing it straight at Elizabeth, he added, "This is no place for young ladies. You need to get yourselves back to your cabin."

"Yes, sir," Elizabeth lowered her head and began pulling Catherine along with her. "We're sorry, sir. We were just curious."

As they pushed past the man, he explained, "They're fixing the boiler. Putting a patch on it. May take all day but had to be done."

Elizabeth didn't answer but kept her head down and moved away as quickly as possible. With Catherine in tow, she scurried down the deck, back up the stairs, and didn't breathe until they had returned to the second deck. She realized she had pushed her luck too far and had put her little sister in danger.

Catching their breath, both girls remained quiet as they thought about the close call. Elizabeth was thinking about what father would do if he found out. Catherine, however, was thinking about something else.

"Will the boat be all right?" she asked with a worried look on her face. "Is the boiler important?"

Afraid that Catherine would be upset and threaten to tell Father about the horrible man, Elizabeth looked at her in surprise. Not appearing to be shaken by the incident at all, the little girl was only concerned about the boat.

"Yes, the boiler is important," Elizabeth began. "It creates steam that causes the boat paddles to move, making the riverboat go."

"But they can fix it, right?" Catherine asked again.

"Yes, they're patching it now," Elizabeth answered. "Once it's patched, it should be fine."

Elizabeth hugged the little girl and added, "And it will get us up north to a new home."

Catherine continued to frown. "And will I like our new home, Bethie?"

"Oh yes," Elizabeth hugged her tighter. "You'll like it very much."

Just then, there was a loud commotion coming from the street at the top of the hill. The two girls watched as a long parade of men slowly descended the cobblestone landing that sloped down to the huge riverboat. It was an unbelievable sight, like walking skeletons rather than men. They were starved, ragged, and filthy. Some were carried along with the help of the stronger ones, bony arms wrapped around equally thin necks. A few of them lying on stretchers looked more dead than alive.

The sisters watched in disbelief as the mob of starved, sickly soldiers shuffled toward the boarding plank. It was incredible that humans could be in such terrible condition and still be living.

"Are these the soldiers Father told us about?" asked Catherine. "What's the matter with them, Bethie?"

"They're sick," Elizabeth said softly. "They've been in prison a long time and not treated very well, it looks like."

As the men approached the boarding plank, Elizabeth could see their hollow eyes and gaunt faces. She could only imagine what they must have been through, all the years of a horrible war, then to be captured and kept in a filthy prison camp not fit for humans. The fact that they even survived was a miracle. But now, here they were, finally boarding a boat to take them home. Their hearts must be bursting with happiness, even though their bodies did not show it.

A wave of guilt suddenly swept over Elizabeth. She had spent the day before fussing over the unwanted passengers and pouting over her lost freedom. Now, here they were, finally going home and earning *real* freedom after months or years of hardship and prison. The very sight of them made Elizabeth feel ashamed.

The mass of soldiers seemed endless as they continued to come down the hill of the landing. Hundreds of them boarded the boat, filling up the decks as they immediately found places on which to lay their blankets. It wasn't until they began coming up the stairs to the cabin deck that Elizabeth stopped staring.

Tugging at Elizabeth's sleeve, Catherine managed to break her sister from the trance she was in.

"Should we go in, Bethie?" Catherine spoke in a nervous little voice. She was afraid of these strange, scary men. "Remember what Father said about the soldiers?"

Surprisingly, the cabin now seemed a welcomed haven from the sights and sounds of the open deck. Elizabeth knew they should be inside as Father had instructed.

"Yes, dear," Elizabeth finally answered. "Yes, let's go in and check on Mother. We can finish reading our story today."

As Elizabeth and Catherine occupied themselves with sewing,

writing lessons, reading, and making up silly songs, soldiers continued to board the *Sultana*. Trainload after trainload poured into the city bringing more starved men who crowded every available space on all the decks. The magnificent steamboat, as great as she was, would be pressed to the limit in getting her passengers home.

Meet Andrew
April 24, 1865

As the train bumped and shook, Andrew prayed that it would not derail as trains on these old, tired rails often did. Crowded in the boxcar like so many cattle going to market were about forty other former prisoners of war. They all had one thing on their minds, home. The war was finally over, and a steamboat was waiting in Vicksburg, just four miles away, to take them home. It was like waking up from an endless nightmare and not fully believing it is over.

For three long years, home had only been a place in Andrew's dreams. As time went on, he feared the faces of his family and the features of his home would fade away. So he practiced making mental pictures of every detail of his loved ones: his mother's hands, his father's eyes, his sisters' hair. In his mind he walked through every room in his house, even bringing back the smells of the kitchen and the fragrances in the garden right outside his window. This game not only kept his memories alive but also helped to distract his mind from the discomforts of long hours in the saddle and sleepless nights on guard duty.

But the only thing that kept him alive during the really horrible, unbearable times was the thought of his love, Mary Louise. He had carried her picture with him through the terrible battle at Stones River in Murfreesboro, Tennessee, a fight that would forever give Andrew nightmares. So many of his fellow soldiers, about 1,300, had died on those frigid days of the new year 1863, and he never understood why he had survived.

Just then, somewhere in the boxcar, a man went into a fit of coughing, a familiar sound that usually meant the man would be found dead the next day and taken out to be buried. At least, that's what had happened in the prison called Cahaba. Until his time at that wretched place, Andrew never dreamed humans could endure such inhumane conditions.

Looking around at all the blank, hollow faces, Andrew knew he would spend a lifetime trying to forget the last six months. But right now, he allowed himself to think on it. It all started when Andrew's company of 3rd Cavalry Tennessee was assigned to the fort at Sulphur Branch Trestle in Alabama. On September 25, 1864, Confederate General Nathan Bedford Forrest's troops attacked the fort. The Union men soon discovered a flaw in the location of the fort, being surrounded by hills from which the enemy could fire down on them. After a hot fight those inside the fort who survived were forced to surrender. They were marched to Cahaba prison, a large open pen near the Alabama River. Being only partially covered, the prison gave little shelter from all the elements of nature. Andrew would never have believed that he could endure such harsh conditions.

All of them were treated more like animals than human beings. It was only by miracle that any of them survived. Living on a daily handful of corn meal, mostly husks, and a few ounces of rancid meat, strong men became weak, sickly skeletons. The Confederacy could not feed their own soldiers with decent food, much less the extra mouths of the Union prisoners. The water for drinking and cooking was so filthy that it caused more sickness and death than the malnutrition. Having been stripped of all their possessions when they entered Cahaba, there were few blankets, and the frigid nights of winter were unbearable.

Somewhere in a corner of the boxcar there came a loud moan, shaking Andrew from his memories. He rose up to see a soldier named Robert from his company holding a friend that lay across Robert's lap. Trying to comfort the poor man, Robert whispered thoughts of home. The dying man's eyes were glazed over, and Andrew knew this one would never see home. Death had surrounded these men for months, and they all could read the signs.

Suddenly, the train jolted the boxcar, knocking the standing men onto those who were sitting. Andrew held his breath and prayed the train hadn't jumped the tracks. It slowed almost to a stop then lurched forward, knocking men over in the opposite direction. As the train began to pick up speed, Andrew breathed a sigh of relief. Maybe they would make it to the boat, after all.

Andrew was surprised at himself. Why wasn't he bursting with excitement? Why was he not thrilled with the prospect of going home? Looking around the crowded boxcar, he watched as men talked, laughed, and nudged one another, and he knew the answer to his question. Andrew missed Elijah, his best friend since early childhood. They had enlisted together as nineteen-year-olds seeking a big adventure. They had fought, ridden, and slept side by side since that day, even trudging into Cahaba prison together. No matter how bad their situation became Elijah could lift Andrew's spirit with his sparkling blue eyes and positive attitude. Elijah could find humor in almost anything.

Until the day the prison flooded, and that changed everything.

When February 1865 rolled around Andrew and Elijah had been in the prison about five months. They had managed to survive by relying on each other, and with a little help from one of the guards. This Confederate guard had taken a liking to Elijah with his blond hair, blue eyes, and funny stories. At times he slipped Elijah a potato or two, a decent loaf of bread, and best of all, a piece of oilcloth to cover the wet, cold ground on which they laid at night. The two friends had also taken possession of two thin, ragged blankets from fellows who were in the cold ground and didn't need them anymore. On those frigid nights Andrew and Elijah would huddle together, wrapped in the blankets, and somehow managed to be alive the next morning.

Then the rains came, without stopping, and the prisoners watched in horror as the Alabama River rose higher each day. As the water crept into the camp, there was no place to escape. A narrow overhang that some of the men had built on one side of the open area to keep out the sun and rain was the only place to get out of the water that became waist high. Taking turns every hour with other prisoners, Andrew and Elijah sat together on the ledge, rubbing their legs and arms to keep warm and telling old stories to distract themselves from their misery. It was more than any human should endure.

After four days with water still filling the prison, several guards in a small boat rowed into the pen and began herding men out the entrance.

"Come on, Elijah," Andrew urged excitedly. "They're letting us leave."

Struggling with all his might to get past other men who were struggling equally hard, Andrew made his way to the gate. In his eagerness to get out of the murky, cold water, he had not noticed that Elijah was not behind him as he thought.

"Elijah! Elijah!" screamed Andrew as he frantically searched the faces around him. By this time he was being pushed and shoved as the mass of men were clamoring to get out. Elijah was nowhere to be seen. Before Andrew knew what was happening, he was carried away with the crowd to higher ground outside the prison and onto dry land. But the pushing mob did not stop there as they were being herded toward wagons that would take them to a waiting train.

As Andrew settled himself in a wagon, there was still no sign of Elijah, and Andrew could only hope his friend was in another wagon. The ride to the train was short, and, once again, Andrew found himself swept off with the crowd and pushed into a boxcar.

Where is Elijah? Andrew repeated again and again in his head. *How did we get separated?* He wished for his friend then more than ever.

No one knew where they were going or how long they would be on the train, but no one cared. They were simply overjoyed to be away from the floodwaters of the camp and the misery it brought; everyone, that is, except Andrew who would have gladly returned to the camp just to find his friend. Andrew knew that if the circumstances were reversed, Elijah would have a positive attitude about seeing Andrew again. As hard as he tried, Andrew couldn't make himself think like Elijah. He couldn't stop his mind from worrying and thinking the worst. He just needed his friend with him.

Once the train stopped and the men were unloaded, Andrew learned more about the situation. They had been carried to a large building in Selma, a few miles away from Cahaba. Only 700 men were allowed to board the trains, leaving the majority of the prisoners back in the pen. In his distress, Andrew had covered the whole building, going from man to man, calling Elijah's name and weeping uncontrollably. Finally collapsing from exhaustion, Andrew had dropped into a corner and had fallen into a fitful sleep. He had lost Elijah.

That day happened a little over a month ago, and he hadn't seen or heard from Elijah since. It was painful to think about. All he could do now as the train pulled into the city was continue to hope he would see his friend again one day.

Soon the train came to a stop. Suddenly, the large door of the boxcar slid open, letting in such bright sunlight that every man covered his face. Grunting and moaning in their efforts to stand up, the former prisoners got their first glimpse of Vicksburg. As they moved down the street toward the river, they gazed in silence at the destruction of the city. It was a harsh reminder of all they had been through the last four years.

Coming over a rise in the street, Andrew and his companions at last saw the great Mississippi River and the giant riverboat that was their ride to freedom. Many men burst into tears, others let out whoops of joy, a few began to sing the "Star Spangled Banner." Andrew just stared in disbelief. As he descended over the cobblestones, he had to watch his shuffling feet carefully so he wouldn't trip and tumble down the slope.

Nearing the boarding plank, he looked up at the beautiful boat. There he saw two girls, one older and the other very young, on the second deck watching this bizarre parade. Shielding his eyes from the sun's glare, he stopped and stared. They were both well dressed and pretty, a sight he had not seen in a very long time. Much to Andrew's surprise, tears welled up in his eyes. With all he had been through, he had seldom cried, but now as he gazed on the young girls, tears rolled down his cheeks. It may have been that they reminded him of a normal life that he thought no longer existed. Or, they may have reminded him of his Mary Louise. Maybe the reality of freedom and home suddenly overwhelmed him. Whatever it was, he could not stop the tears from flowing.

Moving slowly up the boarding plank, Andrew was drawn to the stairs leading to the cabin deck. Standing at the top of the stairs, he looked around and headed to the side of the boat where he had seen the girls. Gone. He searched all around the deck, but the girls were nowhere to be seen.

Of course, thought Andrew. *We scared them into the cabin.*

Then a horrible thought occurred to him.

Am I so wretched that Mary Louise will not want me?

Andrew had not heard from his sweetheart in almost nine months. Although his picture of her had been taken away along with his other things at Cahaba, her lovely face stayed clear in his mind. The thought that she was not waiting for him was too much to bear, and he pushed it from his mind. Right now, he had an important job to do.

While all the other men were busy finding a space on which to settle for the trip, Andrew made his way to the front of the boat. He was determined to examine each man who boarded the boat in hopes of finding Elijah. As each trainload of ex-prisoners passed by, there was no Elijah, and Andrew's optimism began to fade along with the afternoon sun. When the last group came aboard, Andrew's hopes were completely dashed.

With the decks already packed with men, there surely would

be no more trainloads coming. Andrew sighed and turned to leave when something caught his eye. Much to his surprise, he saw another small group of men heading down the landing toward the boat.

Surely they can't be boarding, Andrew thought as he was already being squeezed against the rail by the mass of men now on board. *The boat's already overcrowded now. Where will they put them?*

As Andrew watched the small procession, he guessed that these men were weaker and sicklier than the others. Most of them were being helped along by doctors or carried on stretchers. When they reached the boarding plank, Andrew eyes were fixed on one particular man who was limping on a homemade crutch. His light-colored hair was dirty and in matted clumps, and his head was down as he carefully placed the crutch on the cobblestones. Andrew knew it was not Elijah. It couldn't be. This man was much too thin, and his hair was not the almost-white blond of Andrew's dearest friend. But, for some strange reason Andrew could not take his eyes off the soldier as he struggled up the plank, and, for some even stranger reason, the man suddenly looked up and straight at Andrew.

As soon as he saw the blue eyes gazing out of hollow sockets and dirty face, he knew it was Elijah. Screaming "Elijah", Andrew pushed to get through the crowd. Unable to reach the stairs, he swung both legs over the rail and slid down the post that supported the upper deck. Falling on several men who had settled under the post, Andrew ignored the yells and slaps he received as he pressed on toward the boarding plank.

When he finally reached Elijah, Andrew lifted his friend off the ground in a huge bear hug.

"Whoa," exclaimed Elijah. "Take it easy, my friend."

"Elijah, you're alive!" gasped Andrew excitedly. "You're really alive, and . . . and you're here."

The two friends looked at each other as tears rolled down both their faces. They clasped each other again and wept without shame. Andrew wanted to know every detail of Elijah's journey since the day they were separated, but he also knew they must first find a place for Elijah to lie down. The warmest place Andrew could think of would be near the boilers. This meant pushing their way through the mass of men already covering the deck. It would be difficult, but they would have to try. Elijah was not well. Andrew could see it in his eyes and face; looking at him was almost unbearable.

As they struggled with each step, Andrew held Elijah's sagging body against his own. Suddenly, someone tugged at Andrew's pant leg. Looking down, he saw it was a fellow from his company named Caleb.

"Where you taking your boy there?" he asked in a whisper.

Slightly annoyed, Andrew answered quickly, "We're headed to find a place close to the boilers. Ought to be warm there."

Caleb struggled to get to his feet, grabbed Andrew by the back of the neck, and pulled his head close to him.

"I wouldn't do that if I were you," he glanced around to see if anyone was listening in. "See, I been watching them patch up one of those boilers all afternoon. I know a thing or two about that sort of thing, and just in case that boiler blows, you don't want to be anywhere near it."

Andrew's eyes widened, and he stared at the man with concern. Suspecting Caleb had gone a little mad after all the horrors of war and prison camp, Andrew did not know whether to believe him or not.

"Not saying it's going to happen, mind you," assured Caleb. "But with the overload we got here, this steamboat's going to work harder than she's ever worked before. The patching job wasn't too good, neither." Caleb nodded. "I told you, I know a thing or two about these things."

Andrew gave Caleb a nudge to break his hold and continued to push through the crowded deck.

"Mind you," added Caleb as he sat back down in his spot against the rail.

"What are you thinking?" asked Elijah.

"Well, for one thing, I think Caleb's a little crazy," Andrew managed to smile. "But there's no sense in taking any chances."

So the two friends turned around and made their way toward the front of the boat. They managed to squeeze in between two sleeping comrades with enough room to stretch out their legs.

As the sun went down, and the heavy riverboat slowly pushed away from the dock, Elijah told his story.

Elijah's Story
April 24, 1865

In a hoarse, almost whispering voice, Elijah began his tale of the last two months. Andrew knew his friend was having a hard time breathing, but the cough that frequently stopped Elijah was what concerned Andrew. Sitting beside Elijah now, Andrew made a promise to himself to do everything in his power to get his friend back to health. Once they got home, everything would be all right.

"It was something in the water," Elijah began. "I was right behind you, Andrew—I was."

Elijah rubbed his eyes and then wiped his hand on his pants.

"But I tripped on something sharp in the water," he was shaking his head now. "And down I went under the water. I tried to get up—I tried with all my might, but people just kept pushing me down. They were stepping on me and walking on me. I couldn't get up."

Andrew lifted his arm and placed it around Elijah's shoulders. He was not used to seeing Elijah so sad, and this new emotion was upsetting both of them.

"Then someone pushed me really hard, and I went down again, this time hitting my head on something else in the water," Elijah suddenly started coughing and couldn't stop. Frightened, Andrew tried to sit his friend upright to help him breathe. After a few minutes Elijah caught his breath and leaned back to rest.

"The next thing I knew I was waking up on a dry bed," he continued. "It was Thomas, the guard. You remember him? His name is Thomas." Elijah looked Andrew squarely in the eyes. "You need to know that. He saved my life."

Elijah went on to explain how Thomas had rescued him from drowning in the muddy water and carried Elijah to his own small room. When Elijah woke up, Thomas was cleaning his wound with a little bit of clean water he had in a bucket. It was a bad gash that cut almost to the bone. This made Elijah chuckle.

"That's not saying much, mind you," he pulled up his pant leg to reveal a bony leg, "seeing as I'm just skin and bones to begin with."

Andrew smiled. Every ex-prisoner on this boat was skin and bones, but at least some of them, including Andrew, had a chance to eat better the last two weeks. When news of General Robert

E. Lee's surrender on April 10th reached Selma, the men were transported to a Union holding camp just outside Vicksburg. Elijah had not been so lucky.

After another fit of coughing, Elijah continued to tell how Thomas had searched for something clean to use as a bandage, but not finding anything, Thomas tore his own bed sheet into strips and wrapped the leg tightly to stop the bleeding. Elijah realized then how bad the guards' living conditions were. They had cover at night and a slightly better diet, but not much else.

After three days of hiding out in Thomas's room, Elijah watched the floodwater recede, leaving the pen a sloppy, muddy mess. Andrew and Elijah now looked at each other and laughed. They were remembering a joke between the two of them whenever someone called their prison home a pigpen. Elijah would look at Andrew and say "So what does that make us?" and they would answer together "Pigs!". It always made them laugh even more because it wasn't really funny, just a reason to laugh.

With the waters gone from the camp Elijah had to leave the comfort of Thomas's room and return to the prison yard. Not only did Thomas make him a crutch, but he also made sure Elijah had a spot above the mud on which to lie down. Elijah's cut was very painful, and without proper cleaning, he feared it would get infected. At least once a day, Thomas would sneak by him and douse his wound with a little of his moonshine.

Even so, the leg got worse with time. It swelled and grew red, causing Elijah even more pain. After two weeks, Thomas could not bear to watch Elijah any longer. He brought in a doctor to care for him properly. After examining Elijah's leg, the doctor wanted to cut it off, saying it would save his life. When Elijah refused, the doctor insisted that Thomas and another guard prepare a place for the operation. In most cases wounded men were forced to undergo an amputation whether they wanted it or not. Finding it too unbearable to see Elijah go through such a torturous ordeal, Thomas ordered the doctor to clean and dress the wound then escorted him off the grounds.

"I don't know what you did to make Thomas become such a guardian angel to you," Andrew interrupted the story. "But you were lucky he was there."

Elijah sat quietly for a few minutes, making Andrew a little nervous. Then he rubbed his face and eyes again and continued.

"I reminded him of his son," again Elijah's voice cracked. Andrew knew he was trying not to cry. "Samuel was his name. He was killed at Stones River." Elijah cleared his throat. "He was only seventeen."

Now Andrew understood Elijah's emotions. They had both been at Stones River, and they were both thinking the same thing.

Could one of their bullets have killed Thomas's son Samuel?

It was very unlikely, but not impossible. In such a terrible battle, when the enemy was charging at you, it was kill or be killed. Through heavy smoke and deafening noise, you fired your rifle, saw men fall in front of you, but rarely thought about them as real people with fathers who would grieve over their deaths. So many men had died that day, and the two friends now sat in silence as their thoughts took them back.

After a while Andrew felt Elijah's shoulders begin to shake. The high-spirited boy with a constant smile on his face was now sobbing as if his heart were breaking. As if the floodgates had opened, the tears came pouring out. He was crying for all the death and suffering endured the last four years. He was crying for the poor, pitiful-looking souls on this boat. He was crying because, somehow, they had survived. And he was crying because it was over, and they were going home.

When Elijah calmed down, the two friends sat and listened to the sounds of the big paddlewheel churning up the water as it slowly pushed upstream. They gazed at the stars and fell asleep.

5

Meet Joe
April 26, 1865

The morning wind was chilly, and the rough water of the Mississippi was splashing into the small, dugout boat making Joe wet, cold, and miserable. The boat was no match for the great swollen river, but it was all they had. His father had built the boat to cross from their home on the Arkansas side of the river to Memphis on the eastern bank. The trip across was usually a pleasant float that didn't last long, but with the flooding, it would take twice as long and require some hard paddling.

With aching arms and numb fingers, Joe tried to keep up with the rhythmic strokes of his father's paddle. Pa was sitting with his back to Joe in the front of the boat, and his older brother Daniel was behind him in the rear. Both were paddling with an energy Joe did not have in his twelve-year-old body. His father had big, muscular arms from years of chopping wood and plowing fields, and Daniel had grown to look just like their father. Daniel was Joe's hero.

Now, as he tried to take his mind off his tired arms, Joe thought about the day Daniel left for the war. Being twenty years old at the time, he couldn't be stopped by anyone in the family. His mother wept for days, but Pa was proud of him. Joe missed him terribly. After being captured in the Battle of Shiloh, early in the fighting, Daniel was paroled and forced to sit out the rest of the war. It was a lucky thing for the family, and especially Joe, who adored his older brother.

Just then, a huge log appeared in front of the boat, swirling in an eddy and heading right for them. Pa waved his hand to steer the boat to the right, and both Joe and Daniel switched their paddles to the opposite side of the boat and started paddling frantically. Joe held his breath as the log barely skimmed the side of the boat, tipping it slightly, but moving off in a swirl with the current.

Although it seemed like they had been on the river for hours, the boat had just reached the middle of the stream. One thing that was slowing them down was the awkward raft that was tied to the back of the boat. Pa had used wood planks to build a flat platform with sideboards to haul the supplies he bought at Memphis. When the waves caught the raft, it pulled the boat backwards. As hard as it was to steer the boat now, they were at least going *with* the current in a diagonal line from their home just north of Memphis. Getting back home would be even harder going *against* the current with a loaded raft.

Despite all these discomforts, Joe was excited to be going to the city. News of the arrival of a big riverboat, heavy with a load of sugar, had made Joe anxious to see it. There was also a rumor that many Union ex-prisoners were aboard, and Joe wanted to get a look at a Yankee. Over the years Joe had heard many stories about the terrible, devilish Union men, making them seem to a young boy more like ogres than people.

Joe became so frightened of the Yankees that his mother would talk to him at bedtime about how the soldiers from the North had homes, families, and friends just like they did. She would try to explain how people have different views, and, sadly, how they sometimes settle their disagreements by going to war. These talks usually ended with Ma kissing Joe good night through tears and sniffles, leaving him confused and unable to fall asleep.

Now that he was older and the war was over, Joe was no longer frightened of the Yankees but now very curious. He was sure to see a few of those men today.

Shaken from his thoughts, Joe heard his father shout again. Coming straight at the side of the boat, exactly where Joe was sitting, was a large pile of driftwood and tangled brush. They all

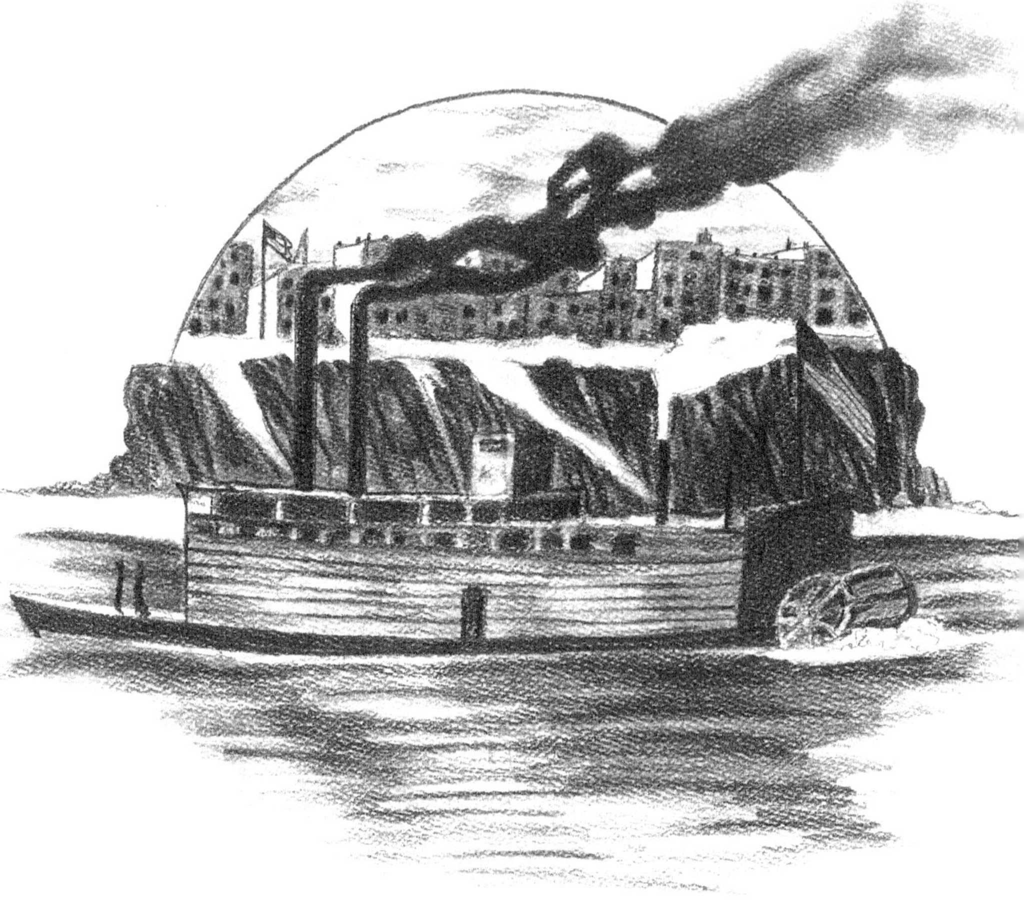

paddled furiously, but they could not escape this time. Daniel was quick to use his paddle to block the pile of wood as it came close to the boat. Straining with all his might, he held the driftwood back as the boat went by. Then he dropped the paddle just as quickly to hold the rope tied to the raft. As the mass of wood rammed into the raft, it jerked the boat and turned it around facing the downstream current, nearly knocking Daniel out of the boat and flipping all of them over. Pa pushed his paddle hard against the swift river, and in a few minutes, they were back on course.

All this motion had set their small boat rocking dangerously. Flashing before his mind's eye, Joe saw himself thrown in the water. The thought of going into the cold, churning, muddy current had always been his worst nightmare. The Mississippi was a treacherous river, and those who lived along it had a fearful respect for it.

When the scary moment passed, Joe realized he had dropped his paddle at his feet and was gripping the sides of the little boat as tightly as he could. His fear had caused him to freeze and made him unable to help either Daniel or his father save the situation. Ashamed that he had not jumped into action like his brother and father, Joe wished he could be as brave and strong as they were.

"Everybody all right?" Pa asked without turning to look back. He could not take his eyes off the river or his paddle.

"Yes, sir," called Joe. His floppy-brimmed hat was pulled down so far on his head that he could barely see out from under it. He tilted his head back and looked down his nose to see ahead.

Much to his relief, the dark shoreline was now beginning to look like a city. The buildings were taking shape, and Joe could see the outline of several boats docked at the landing. It wouldn't be long now. Maybe they *would* make it to Memphis without capsizing. Joe relaxed just a little as he continued to paddle hard. He really had begun to think that they wouldn't make it, and his tight stomach made him feel sick.

It was close to noon when Pa, Daniel, and Joe finally got the boat docked, and the raft tied down. Joe loved all the activity going on; all the busy people, the boats of different sizes, some docking, others pulling away. But he was disappointed that the giant riverboat *Sultana* wasn't here yet.

"Looks like we got a little time," Pa said as he spread out a large piece of cloth on the cobblestones. "We might as well have lunch. Your ma packed us some really good eats."

Pa unwrapped some ham, a jar of pickled eggs, and a few biscuits from breakfast. Seeing the food, Joe realized how hungry he was, now that they were safe on the bank and his nervous stomach had settled down, so he dug in. Daniel did not join them, however, as he had urgent business and needed to be on his way. He promised to meet Pa back at the dock in a few hours to help load the supplies.

As Daniel made his way up the landing and disappeared down the street, Pa and Joe smiled at each other. They both knew that Daniel had a sweetheart on Jefferson Street, and she was his *urgent business*. Soon Pa saw a friend and went to talk with him, leaving Joe to finish up a second biscuit alone.

As Joe sat looking out over the river, he saw a dark spot on the horizon. Though it was just a speck at first, it grew larger as he watched. Flipping his hat brim out of his face, he kept his eye on the object, and he realized that it was a riverboat coming toward Memphis. As it neared, he could see that it was a very large riverboat with something on the decks.

That's strange, thought Joe.

He had never seen a steamboat with cargo stored on all the decks before.

How were the passengers supposed to walk on the deck with all that stuff? Joe was puzzled. *This is very strange.*

Squinting from the sun, he began to see the features of the boat as it pushed through the water toward him, the stairs between the decks, the smokestacks, the pilothouse. Then his jaw dropped as he realized what was on the decks of the *Sultana*. It wasn't cargo at all—but people.

As the boat pulled in and docked, Pa came up behind Joe.

"Woo-ie!" Pa exclaimed. "I never saw so many people on one boat in all my life."

Not taking his eyes off the fantastic sight, Joe stared in awe.

"Me neither," Joe whispered. "How come they got so many men on her, anyway?"

Joe turned to his father and added, "Won't she sink with all that weight?"

"You'd think so," Pa replied. "But I guess they know what they're doing. I don't know, son, looks bad to me, too."

Father and son both stared in disbelief at the sight. After a few minutes of silence, Pa left to talk to a man about some pigs and buy the supplies.

"Now, Joe," Pa instructed before he went. "You stay with our boat. That's your job, you hear? Don't want nobody messing with our things, so you got to stay put." He put a hand on Joe's shoulder. "I know you will."

"Yes, Pa," Joe said with a nod and a smile. "I'll stay right here till you get back."

"When Daniel and I return," he continued, "we'll get some sugar from the *Sultana* to take home."

Joe smiled and settled down on a seat in their boat. He knew he had a long afternoon ahead, but he didn't care. There was a lot going on here, so he wouldn't be bored.

When the *Sultana* was docked and tied securely, the cargo and boarding planks were lowered. People began to move, and as they disembarked, Joe got to see the Yankees—not just a few, but more than he could imagine. These men were scary, but not in a way that frightened him when he was younger. They looked like skeletons as they stumbled and shuffled down the plank. Joe could see their sunken faces and hollow eyes. He had never seen humans so thin with their ragged, dirty clothes hanging off their bodies. It reminded Joe of himself when he tried wearing Daniel's coat or shirt. Joe couldn't imagine what these men had gone through to be in such a condition. Watching them now, he felt only pity, nothing more.

Though the ex-prisoners who did leave the boat were thin and weak, they were still able to do so. There were others who could not get up from their blankets on the decks to see the town or get a good meal. These poor souls lined the decks that had gradually thinned out, and they were now holding Joe's attention.

At that moment, it happened.

Looking up at the second deck, Joe glimpsed the most beautiful girl he had ever seen. There she was, standing by the rail, among the dirty Union men, looking out at the river. Joe could not take his eyes off her.

At first, he didn't think she was real. He thought his eyes were playing tricks on him. He couldn't understand why a girl so well dressed and pretty would be among so many miserable men. She couldn't be real.

Then suddenly the girl looked down at his boat, his raft, and then straight at Joe. They stared at each other for several minutes until Joe became embarrassed and pulled his hat down over his eyes, turning away. He waited only a few seconds before looking back, and when he did, she was gone. His eyes scoured the deck, right and left, but there was no sign of her.

Had she really been there? thought Joe, doubting his own eyes. *'Yes, of course, she was there. She was real. She had looked directly at me.*

Now Joe was no longer thinking about the sad men in blue. His mind was thinking only of the girl who had stared at him with eyes that were blue.

The Plan
April 26, 1865

"No, no, and no more!" Father had said in a thunderous voice. "It is enough, Elizabeth!"

Last night and all this morning Elizabeth was relentless in her begging to go ashore when they arrived in Memphis. When the riverboat left Vicksburg two days ago, she had stayed in the cabin without an argument. The decks became so crowded with over two thousand ex-prisoners that she felt safe within the walls of their small room.

But a whole day of confinement had worn on her nerves. Catherine and Elizabeth had played every game she knew, read their books more than once, practiced their needlepoint, and became hoarse from singing too long. By the time night fell, Elizabeth started to plead with her father.

Although Father's heart was aching to please his daughter, he remained hard as stone on his decision that she stay in the cabin. He had no other choice under the circumstances of the overcrowded boat. Father was annoyed with the unwanted passengers, Dee was annoyed with Elizabeth for stirring up trouble, and Elizabeth was annoyed with both men for denying her the freedom they enjoyed. The tensions at supper were very high.

Later, as Elizabeth lay on her couch bed, she was determined to think of a plan. The sneaking out with Catherine on the decks at Vicksburg hadn't been discovered, but Elizabeth knew better than to include her little sister in any more of these adventures. She would have to think of a way to leave Catherine and Mother in the cabin while she went out for a breath of fresh air. Tossing and turning on the uncomfortable bed, she listened to the noises of the men right outside her window. Their coughing was endless, and the occasional shouts and bursts of laughter made it impossible to sleep. She felt even more irritated with the intruders and became more determined to get out on the decks despite them.

By morning she had yet to think of a way to shed her family and this stifling little room, and she was in a foul mood. As soon as Father and Dee entered for breakfast, she started her pleading again, only to send Father into a rage, storming out of the room into his own cabin. Then Dee became outraged as well and stormed out after him.

Now the great riverboat was pulling into the dock at Memphis, and Elizabeth would not be enjoying the sights of the bustling city. She sat in the chair and pouted as Father and Dee came to say their good-byes to Mother and Catherine. They simply looked at Elizabeth and sighed as they closed the door behind them.

Seeing the door close made Elizabeth even more miserable. She decided to sit in the chair all day, puff up like an old toad, and refuse to speak or even smile. This would, of course, make Mother and Catherine miserable, too. Right now, Elizabeth didn't care. If she was going to be treated like a child, she would act like one.

The small cabin room felt even smaller as Elizabeth's mood worsened. When Mother asked her to comb Catherine's hair, Elizabeth snapped at her. When Catherine fidgeted while having her hair combed, Elizabeth scolded her severely. Seeing the looks of hurt on both their faces made Elizabeth feel even more miserable. Both mother and younger sister retreated to the bed to get out of her way. And Elizabeth curled up in the chair to pout some more.

After a few minutes Mother and Catherine set aside their book and fell asleep for an afternoon nap. Tired of sulking all by herself, Elizabeth decided to step into the hallway to stretch her legs.

As she opened the door and stepped out, the loud performing group with the gaudy clothes came barreling out of their rooms down the hall. This time they were carrying bags and pulling trunks. It was their final stop as they were giving a performance at a Memphis theatre tonight. How Elizabeth envied them and their freedom!

As the group passed Elizabeth, the men tipped their hats to her, and the women said "ta-ta" in high-pitched, dramatic voices as they flipped their flashy boas at her. One actress with heavy rouge and lipstick touched Elizabeth on the chin and commented, "What a pretty thing you are!"

At that moment a surprising thing happened. As the rowdy bunch headed for the outside door, without thinking, Elizabeth moved right along with them. It was as if the performers had swept her away with them, and she could not help herself. The door opened, and they all burst into the sunlight.

Stepping over blankets, clutter, and live bodies lying on the deck, the actors headed for the stairs and off the uncomfortable boat. Heading in the opposite direction, Elizabeth stepped carefully as she made her way toward the rail. Although many men had gone ashore and some of the stronger ones were unloading the boat to earn a little money, there were still a lot of men on the deck. Elizabeth could feel the gawking eyes on her as she passed, and it made her extremely nervous. She suddenly felt very alone and unprotected. She wished Dee were with her now to help her get through the maze of men and their unwanted attention.

Yet she kept going.

To be able to look out on the river and take in a deep breath of fresh air made it worth the stares and the calls to her. Focusing on her feet so she wouldn't step on a hand or a leg, she finally made it to the rail. What a glorious sight it was!

The river had risen almost to the roads, covering most of the landing and bringing the docked boats closer to the streets of the town. Elizabeth could see horses, buggies, and people from her perch on the second deck. Oh how she wished she could be there with them!

Turning away from the scene that made her feel left out, she concentrated on the view of the river instead. It was a mighty force, pushing huge logs along as if they were tiny twigs. She was reminded of Dee's warnings about falling in, and although she laughed at him then, she knew how terrible that would be and secretly feared the cold, cruel water.

For some reason, Elizabeth took her eyes off the river and looked down. There below the giant riverboat she saw a small, very strange-looking boat with an even stranger-looking raft tied beside it. Sitting in the boat was a young boy, wearing a most ridiculous hat with a floppy brim that hung down over his face, a loose shirt, and worn-out pants. Elizabeth realized that, as she was staring at this boy, he was also staring at her. They locked eyes for a few minutes before he pulled his hat down even lower and looked away.

That's it! thought Elizabeth to herself. *That's the plan!*

The boy had given her a brilliant idea, and she was off to get it started.

The Great Escape
April 26, 1865

Spinning around, Elizabeth lifted her long, full skirt slightly to allow her feet to step quickly and carefully over the clutter on the deck. She didn't have much time. Father and Dee would return in less than three hours so she had to hurry.

"Where you going, missy?" a voice called from somewhere on the deck. "Stay a little longer, won't you?"

Another voice muttered something Elizabeth couldn't hear, and both men laughed. She paid them no mind. Now she felt braver as she moved among these men; she had a plan.

Once inside the quiet hallway of the cabins Elizabeth breathed easier. She stepped lightly as she moved past each cabin door. When she reached her own, she stopped. Holding her breath, she laid her ear against the door. Not a sound could be heard within the room, and Elizabeth could only hope both Mother and Catherine were still asleep. She didn't dare open the door to be sure but moved quickly to Father and Dee's room.

Once inside the men's cabin, she scanned the room for Dee's suitcase. There, at the end of the couch, which was also Dee's bed, was the bag. Picking through Dee's clothes very carefully so he would not become suspicious, Elizabeth found a pair of pants and a shirt. She quickly exchanged her blouse and skirt for her brother's clothes.

Shoes, thought Elizabeth. *What about shoes?*

She had failed to consider her feet, but that would not stop her. Looking around the room, Elizabeth spied a pair of old boots. Unlacing her own high-top shoes, she slipped the boots on and laced them up. Unlike the clothes that fit fairly well, the shoes were too big. She would just have to make the best of it.

Now for the hair. Again, she looked around until she found several of Dee's hats. The formal, high-top hats would never do, and she was becoming frustrated until she saw a flat, billed cap that looked like one a younger boy would wear.

Perfect! Elizabeth thought as she pushed her netted hair up into the cap.

Taking a quick glance in the mirror Elizabeth gasped and then laughed. She did not recognize herself, and this pleased her immensely. She pulled her shoulders back, took a deep breath, and headed for the door.

Before leaving, though, she found a piece of paper and a pen. Scribbling a short note to Mother, Elizabeth explained she was in Father's room writing in her journal and didn't want to be disturbed. After her bad behavior earlier, she knew neither Mother nor Catherine would dare come see about her.

As she passed their room, she slipped the note under the door. Now that her mood was lifted, she felt really ashamed about how she had treated them. She knew she would have to apologize to both of them before the day was over.

It was impossible not to clunk down the hall in the oversized boots, but Elizabeth was trying her best to set her feet down as softly as possible. Her heart was racing as she pushed open the outside door. Slipping out as quickly as possible, she took a few steps and looked around. No one seemed to have noticed that she came from the cabin area. Better yet, no one seemed to notice her at all.

Wanting to race down the stairs, Elizabeth had to control herself and move slowly. Her clumsy gait was very similar to the walk of many of the weak ex-prisoners, and this was another advantage for her. Moving carefully down the stairs, she made it to the first deck where all the activities of loading and unloading were going on.

Elizabeth stepped inside a doorway to keep from being knocked out of the way and planned her next move. She was thrilled that no one took any notice of her, and this made her even braver. But she had to stay as invisible as possible. Elizabeth could see that going down the boarding plank might draw attention to herself because there were very few people getting off by this time.

Deciding to use the cargo plank, Elizabeth made her way along the deck, dodging men carrying boxes and pulling carts, until she reached the plank. She waited for just the right moment when she could slip by, then moved between a cart piled high with boxes and a man leading a hog. After a few steps, her feet finally touched land. How wonderful it felt to be free of the boat at last!

Not hesitating a minute longer, Elizabeth knew exactly where she was going. With head down, she moved through the crowd until she rounded the front of the big riverboat and made it to the opposite side.

Good, she thought. *He's still there.*

The young boy was still sitting in the little boat, and Elizabeth went right up to him.

"Hi," she said, startling him so badly that he jumped.

The boy stared at Elizabeth for a few minutes, trying to figure out who this strange boy was. He did not recognize her at all, and again this made Elizabeth smile.

"Hi," Joe finally answered, not knowing what else to say.

"My name's Elizabeth," she laughed out loud to see the look on the boy's face. "From up on the deck." She pointed as she spoke.

Joe was so confused that he couldn't speak. The person on the deck was a beautiful girl, not this *boy*.

"What's your name?" She continued to prod the boy to speak.

Finally, Joe found his voice and answered, "Name's Joe. But you . . . you can't be the girl. Are you?"

He was studying her face carefully. And then his eyes got big, and his mouth dropped open. It was the eyes. Yes, those were the beautiful blue eyes he had seen. But what was she doing dressed like a boy? This made no sense.

"May I sit with you?" she asked politely.

Again, Joe could only nod and point to the board that made a crude seat. Looking around to see if anyone was watching, Joe could not hide his nervousness as the girl came closer. He had a thousand questions for her, but the words would not come out.

Seeming to forget about Joe, Elizabeth lifted her head, closed her eyes, and breathed in the fresh air. Joe peered at her from under his broad hat. Even dressed like this, she was still beautiful.

Suddenly Elizabeth stared right at Joe causing him to jump again and blurt out, "Why are you dressed like that?"

Elizabeth laughed out loud at this shy, funny boy named Joe.

"It was the only way I could sneak away," she explained. "After all these men boarded at Vicksburg, Father would not permit me to leave the stuffy cabin. It was unbearable."

Seeing that he was still confused, she continued, "Father and my brother Dee have gone into town. Mother and my little sister are sleeping. You gave me the idea. It was my chance."

"Where are you going?" asked Joe, his curiosity now growing bigger than his shyness.

"We're headed to Illinois," Elizabeth smiled dreamily. "The man I'm going to marry is there."

For some strange reason Joe felt a tiny prick in his heart when he heard this. He couldn't explain it, but he felt disappointed.

"What's his name?" Joe asked and then realized it was a dumb question. What difference did it make?

"Oh," Elizabeth looked surprised. "I don't know his name. I haven't met him yet." She smiled again. "But I know he's there."

All Joe could think was that girls sure get strange when they get older.

There was silence as Joe lowered his head and thought about this. When he looked from under his hat at Elizabeth again, she was staring at him with an intent expression on her face. He blushed and looked away.

"Do you want to go walking with me?" she finally said, her

eyes twinkling with excitement.

Joe was surprised.

"Can't," he replied. Then added, "Pa said to stay here and watch the boat."

Elizabeth looked at him curiously.

"Do you always do as you're told?" she bent down to see his face under the floppy brim.

If his heart had been pricked a few minutes ago, now his pride was crushed. This girl sure did strange things to his feelings.

"Yep, I guess I do," he stammered, now reduced to feeling like a six-year-old.

Elizabeth sat quietly. The wheels of her mind were turning with ways to get the boy to go with her.

It was Joe who broke the silence, trying to change the subject.

"Why is your family on this boat with all these men anyway?" he asked.

Elizabeth sighed and answered, "We boarded in New Orleans, and what a wonderful trip it was until we reached Vicksburg."

Elizabeth explained how Father tried to get his money back and put the family on a different boat, but the captain wouldn't do it.

Joe listened with great interest and then asked, "Did you live in New Orleans?" It sounded like an exciting place to someone who hadn't been anywhere but Memphis.

"No, but not far from there in Louisiana."

"You see any gators where you lived?" Now here was a subject Joe was interested in, and it showed on his face.

Elizabeth's eyes lit up with the idea that just hit her. She knew how to get the boy to go with her.

"Lots of them!" Then she added. "You want to see one?"

"Here?" Joe looked surprised. "There's no gators here."

"Oh, yes there is," Elizabeth grinned. "I'll show you if you want, but you'll have to leave your boat. I can't bring it to you."

She prodded a little more. "If you dare, that is."

Elizabeth watched Joe carefully and waited for his response. He was seriously thinking about it, so she made it even more enticing.

"It's a big one, almost seven feet long," Elizabeth said with much enthusiasm. "And it's right there on the *Sultana*."

This was more than Joe could bear. He would risk his pa's anger and possibly a few licks from his strap to see a real, live gator. And what a story he would have for his friends!

So Elizabeth and Joe headed back to the front of the riverboat and around to the cargo plank. Elizabeth was whispering instructions to her new companion on how to sneak up the plank and head to the back of the boat to a large storage room. She led him inside a wide door and there, under a set of stairs, was a real, live alligator in a huge, wooden crate. Elizabeth explained how it belonged to the crew, and they had named it *The General*.

Joe was speechless as he gawked at the creature. He walked all around the crate and studied every inch of the large gator. Urging him to stick his hand through the slats to touch the tail, Elizabeth laughed loudly at the way Joe jerked his hand back after feeling the tough skin.

Joe could have watched *The General*, just lying there for hours, but Elizabeth had other plans, and the clock was ticking.

"Let's go, Joe," Elizabeth urged. "We need to leave."

Snapping out of his gator trance, Joe agreed.

"Yeah, Pa may be back and looking for me."

But that's not what Elizabeth had in mind. Oh no, not at all.

"First go with me to the street," Elizabeth said. "Just for a few minutes. I want to get a look. I promise we won't stay long."

Joe began shaking his head *no* when Elizabeth took him by the shoulders and looked him straight in the face.

"Listen, you've already disobeyed your pa. Right?"

Joe had to nod in agreement.

"We're both going to be punished if our fathers find out," she stated the obvious. "So what's ten more minutes to see the city?"

Joe was thinking on this but not yet convinced.

"Aren't you tired of being left out of the fun?"

Now Elizabeth hit a nerve, and the boy's face tightened. He was thinking about always being left to watch the boat while Pa and Daniel went off to enjoy the city.

She was right. Somehow this strange girl had a way of explaining things that made sense to Joe. It didn't seem wrong when she put it that way. What difference would ten more minutes make? And the sights they would see made it worth the risk.

So off went the two "boys" to see the city.

8

A Close Call
April 26, 1865

Two pairs of legs were burning from the steep climb up the cobblestone street that led to the top of the bluff on which the city of Memphis was built. The oversized boots didn't help the situation for Elizabeth, and she was gasping for breath as they neared the top. It also didn't help that Joe had tired out halfway up the hill, and she was pulling him along to keep up. There was so much to see and so little time. Her body was tingling with excitement, and they were not moving quickly enough.

When they reached the top, they stopped at the corner to catch their breath.

"Okay," Joe was trying to speak between big gasps. "Okay, we're here. Let's go now."

Elizabeth looked at him as if he had grown a second head.

"Are you blind?" she exclaimed. "This is Front Street. Can't you see there's nothing here but old cotton warehouses and offices and . . . and old men with cigars."

Then she pointed ahead past the next block.

"That's where we want to be," her eyes twinkled as she spoke. "That must be Main Street. That's where all the excitement is."

Giving Joe a nudge on his shoulder and grabbing his shirt sleeve, she pulled him across the street and up the next block. At least the streets were level now, and the walking was easier.

Joe didn't argue. He knew he was in way over his head, so he might as well make the most of it. He was sure it was just a matter of time before he met the wrath of his pa and some stinging licks. His mother would cry, and Daniel would shake his head, questioning his little brother's character. Wishing he were still sitting in his boat, Joe was trying to figure out how he got into this mess. It had all happened so quickly.

Then, quite suddenly, Elizabeth stopped pulling on his arm, and Joe looked out from under his hat to see a most wonderful sight. Standing on the corner of Main Street outside a small general store, they had an open view of all the activities going on. People were moving here and there, going in and out of dining halls and shops, and passing by on horseback or in buggies. Joe had never seen anything like it. Pa had never brought him to Main Street before, and his eyes couldn't take it all in quickly enough. Yes, it was worth the trouble he was going to be in.

Outside the general store were barrels of pickles, flour, and crackers, and the two travelers stood behind these as they watched the street. Good smells of freshly baked bread and cinnamon cakes coming from the store reminded both of them how hungry they were. So many good things to eat; but with no money, all of it was out of their reach and their stomachs.

Elizabeth was straining to see everything she could possibly see up and down the street when she spied two young girls about her age. They were walking straight toward her, and Elizabeth couldn't take her eyes off them. *How fine their dresses are! And those bonnets, oh how lovely they are!* Suddenly she wished she were in her own clothes, walking proudly down the street, giggling as they were doing, and stopping to *ooh* and *aah* at the shop windows.

When the girls came close to Elizabeth and Joe, one of them covered her mouth with her fan and whispered something to her friend. Giggling loudly, they stole glances at the two awkward "boys" and giggled even more. As they passed, the two young girls looked back over their shoulders with looks of ridicule. In those few moments, the bubble of excitement burst, and Elizabeth felt her face flush with embarrassment. She wanted to stomp her foot and scream at the snooty girls, but she was forced to let them pass without a word.

Watching the girls move down the street, Elizabeth huffed in frustration and spun around to face Joe. That's when her heart stopped.

There, coming down the street in their direction, was Father and Dee. Elizabeth yanked on Joe's shirt, pulling him down behind the barrels.

"What'd you do that for?" Joe yelped.

"Sh-h-h-h," Elizabeth hissed between her teeth. "It's Father! And Dee. They're coming. They're headed right for us!"

Elizabeth's head was spinning, and she felt like she might faint. But that would only draw attention to herself. She had to stay calm and think of some way to escape. If the two of them ran, they might be mistaken for thieves and chased by an officer. That would surely get them noticed. If they moved casually back toward the boat, Father and Dee would most likely see them. Although Elizabeth was certain they wouldn't recognize her, Dee would know the clothes, especially the hat. She felt like a rat caught in a trap and was about to panic.

"Stand up, Joe," she ordered. "See how close they are now."

"But how will I know them?" asked Joe in a weak voice. This headstrong girl who had been in control all afternoon was now in trouble and no longer had a plan. Joe did not know what to do, and it was scaring him.

Elizabeth quickly described her father and brother then pushed Joe on his feet. As soon as his head popped up from behind the barrel, he saw them. They were only three stores away and moving on. Elizabeth bit her lip in an effort to think harder.

"Wait," Joe said. "They're stopping. Yes, they're looking at something in a shop window."

Joe was quiet for a few minutes.

"Looks like a ladies' shop." Joe paused. "They're going in."

That's all Elizabeth needed to hear. Without any warning, she jumped up and began walking as rapidly as she could back to Front Street. When Joe realized she had left him, he hustled to catch up. Reaching the corner of Front Street, Elizabeth dared to look back to see if Father and Dee had turned the corner. No sign of them yet. So she pushed on across the street with Joe trying hard to keep up.

The steep descent to the landing and the riverboat slowed them down considerably as they had to push their feet against the slope to keep from running out of control. At least now they were hidden from the level streets above and would not be spotted if Father and Dee rounded the corner on Main Street.

At last Elizabeth and Joe reached the *Sultana*, and with a quick good-bye, Elizabeth scooted once again to the cargo plank. By this time of day, there weren't many men unloading things, so

Elizabeth grabbed a box from the ground. Lifting it in front of her face, she scurried up the plank. Just as quickly, she dropped the box and moved along the deck. Pushing her way through crowds of men, she made it to the stairs and started up.

Thinking only of getting to Father's cabin and her own clothes, she did not see the men at the top of the stairs. With a thud, she smacked into someone and fell flat on her back. The impact sent her hat flying off her head, breaking the net that held back her hair. Her long black hair billowed out.

Elizabeth was horrified. She could feel the stares of the shocked men around her. The silence was even worse.

Looking up to see what had knocked her down, Elizabeth stared into the stunned faces of two Union soldiers, both young but thin, dirty, and sickly-looking. One man was holding up his friend who had a bandaged leg and used a crutch. Their eyes were big with surprise. Despite the panic Elizabeth was in, she noticed how blue the injured one's eyes were. With not a minute to waste, Elizabeth scrambled to her feet, grabbed the hat, and flew inside the cabin doorway.

In only a few minutes, Elizabeth had changed into her own clothes, being careful to pack Dee's things away exactly as he had left them. Before leaving, she checked the room to see if anything was out of place. Then she took a deep breath to calm her body and prepared to face Mother and Catherine.

As Elizabeth stepped into the room, Catherine leapt across the floor and wrapped her arms around her sister's waist. As they hugged, Elizabeth could feel something hard against her back as Catherine looked up at her with urgency. Catherine was trying to push the object into Elizabeth's hands. Just then, Elizabeth remembered the note she had written, the one that said she was in Father's cabin writing in her journal. Catherine was now pressing that journal on Elizabeth. Her little sister didn't know what Elizabeth had done, but Catherine knew Elizabeth had done *something* to disobey Father and was trying to save her big sister from punishment. Leaving the journal in her own cabin was a detail that had slipped by Elizabeth, and the mistake could have unraveled her whole plan. She would have to thank her sister later for helping with the cover-up.

It wasn't until night, as Elizabeth lay in the dark on her couch, that she thought of Joe. She was wondering now if his pa had caught him, or if he had been lucky to return without being discovered as well. Thinking back, she wasn't even sure why she had included the boy in her adventure. Perhaps she wasn't as brave as she liked to believe. All her life she had Dee or Father watching over her, escorting her wherever she went, and although she sometimes fumed about the restrictions, she felt uncomfortable without a male companion.

Elizabeth knew she would never see the boy again, but they had spent a day together that neither one of them would ever forget. She smiled as she fell asleep.

It was around eleven o'clock when the *Sultana* pushed back from the dock and began her last few hours on the great river. While Elizabeth slept and dreamed about her adventure, the giant riverboat strained under the weight of its overload. While Andrew and Elijah slept on the front of the middle deck, having talked about the beautiful girl and her wavy black hair until they dropped off to sleep, the overworked boilers pushed the heavy vessel against the downstream current. While Joe slept in his loft bed on the western bank of the river, after soaking his red whelps from Pa's strap but still smiling as he dreamed about his exciting day, the *Sultana* passed slowly by like a huge dark shadow.

9

River of Fire
April 27, 1865, 2:00 a.m.

The sound was like the loudest boom of thunder ever heard. At the same time Elizabeth felt a sharp pain in her shoulder and an even sharper one on her head. She awoke to find herself across the small cabin room on the floor under something wooden and heavy. In the dark it was impossible to see what had happened. She lay motionless as she tried to clear her sleepy mind.

Then she heard the screams of her mother and Catherine. That was the spark she needed to pull herself out from under the table that had pinned her down. Finally getting on her feet, Elizabeth realized the room was filled with steam, making it hard to breathe.

Before she could take a step, Father and Dee burst into the room, letting in more steam and heat.

"We've got to get out," yelled Father. Elizabeth had never seen him in such distress. "Hurry, dears, hurry. We must get out."

There was no time to wonder what was happening. She stumbled over a chair in her efforts to reach Catherine but somehow, found the child on the floor. Scooping up the little girl and holding her close to her body, Elizabeth moved to the door. Catherine was clinging to Elizabeth with all her might. In the darkness and the steam, Elizabeth stumbled and almost fell. A strong hand grabbed her arm. It was Dee. With Father behind them holding Mother, the family stepped into the hallway.

It was an astonishing sight! Elizabeth was overwhelmed, and for a few minutes, everyone forgot about escaping and stared in complete shock.

At the other end of the hallway, just past Father's room, one of the giant smokestacks had crashed through the ceiling and was lying above a huge hole in the floor. The rooms at the other end of the hall seemed to have disappeared as there was nothing but a huge crater. Through the gaping hole they could see the lower deck where a fire was gaining strength. As she was pulled down the hallway by Dee and pushed from behind by Father, she couldn't help but think about the people who had been in the rooms or fallen below in the fire.

Before they reached the outer door, Father put a jacket of some kind on Catherine and herself, pulling the straps tightly around them. She knew it was a flotation device, and a terrible fear gripped her.

Will I have to jump in the water?

The thought of the cold, churning water paralyzed her, and she could not make her feet move. There was no way she could jump in the river. She couldn't swim, yet she knew she couldn't stay on a boat that was burning. For the first time in her life, Elizabeth was terrified beyond reason.

When Dee opened the door to the outside deck, the scene was one of total frenzy, men pushing and shoving, some screaming or crying, others praying or cursing. Panicking, large groups of people were leaping over the sides into the darkness and cold water.

"Hold on to me," Dee yelled above the noise. "Don't let go, no matter what."

With one arm wrapped around Catherine and the other gripping Dee's arm, Elizabeth followed her brother through the madness toward the front of the boat.

By this time, the fire in the rear of the riverboat was so bright it lit up the night sky as if it were day. Reaching the rail, Elizabeth looked over to see another unbelievable sight. The river was alive with people!

Panicked men were grabbing at each other and anything that would float. Some were fighting over a small board or box. Those who could swim were being pulled down by those who could not.

To try to swim in the chaotic water would be a death trap.

Dee took control again.

"We have to stay calm and stay put," he tried to sound calm himself, but his voice gave away his fears. He looked back at the fire. "At least, as long as we can."

Then Dee realized that their parents were not behind them. He yelled for Father as he searched the crowd. They were nowhere in sight. At that moment, Dee knew he was responsible for his sisters' safety, and this scared him more than the fire or the water.

As Elizabeth watched the horrible scene around her, she spied the two soldiers who had earlier knocked her down. Unlike the other men, they did not appear to be panicked but were moving together with a purpose. The healthy friend was carrying a board about five feet long, followed by the blue-eyed one with his crutch. When they got to the rail, the wounded soldier dropped his crutch and held the board as the other one slipped over the rail and out of sight. Then his friend lifted the board over the rail until it dropped to the man below. Managing to get his bandaged leg over the rail, he followed the other and disappeared into the darkness.

Somehow, watching these two soldiers work together to save themselves calmed Elizabeth's fears. It may not be hopeless, after all, and she began to pray, just pray, for that's all she could do.

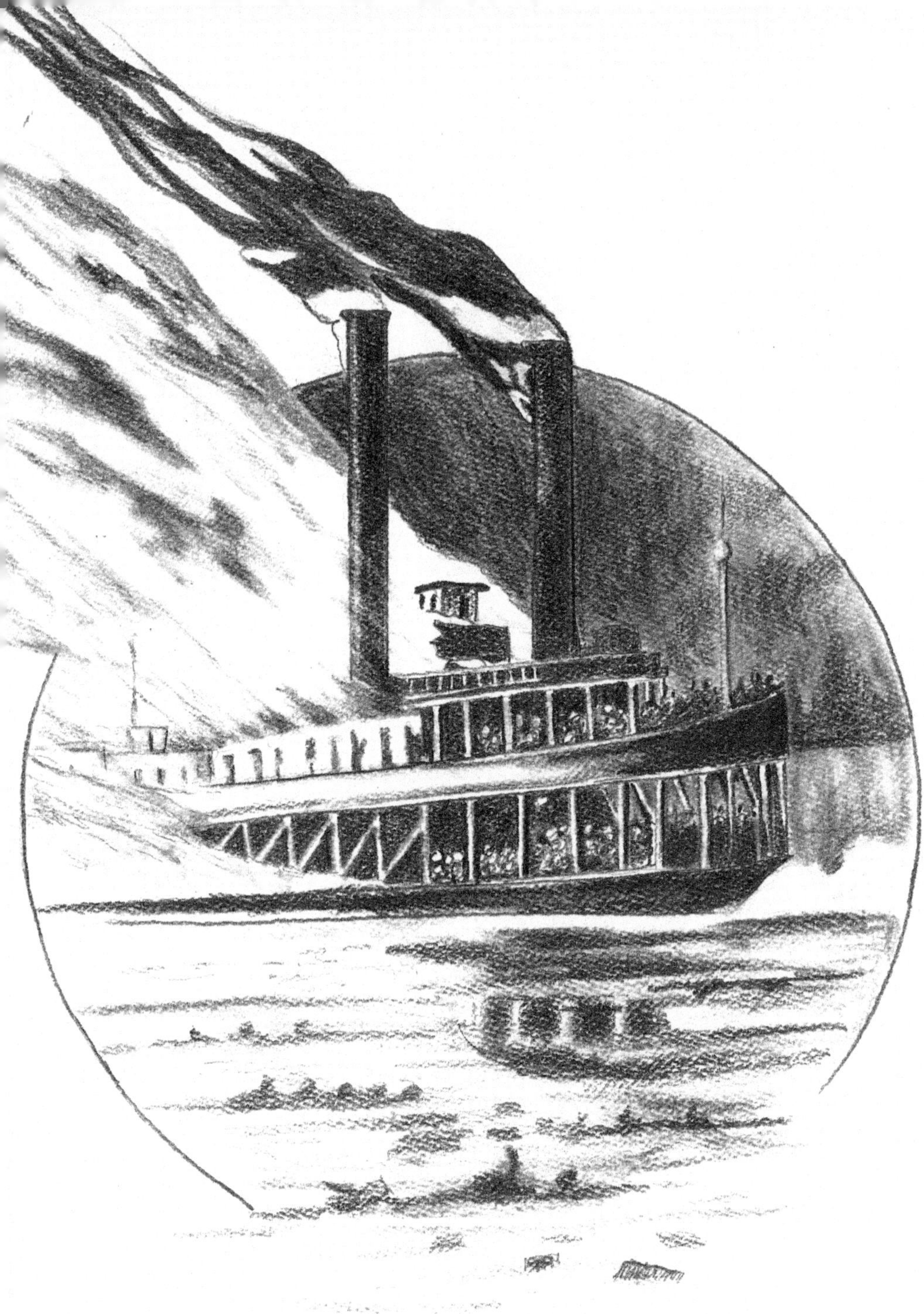

10

An Unexpected Rescue
April 27, 1865, 2:00 a.m.

When Andrew heard the loud, thunderous boom, he awoke with a start. Groping for his rifle, he believed he was on a battlefield again with the enemy's cannon firing at him. As his head began to clear, he looked around and remembered where he was. Unaware of anything happening, Elijah slept soundly next to him. Andrew shook his friend to wake him up just as he heard a loud crash and saw one of the giant smokestacks falling across the huge riverboat.

Quickly, Andrew helped Elijah to his feet to keep them from being trampled as the crowd became excited. Men were pushing and screaming as they watched the flames grow higher. The two friends could see that the dark waters were becoming alive with hundreds of desperate people, drowning each other in their efforts to save themselves. It was no time to panic, but it was hard to stay calm.

"What'll we do, Andrew?" Elijah said in his hoarse voice then coughed deeply.

Andrew didn't answer right away. He was thinking on it. They hadn't survived all the hardships and come this far to be pulled down into the muddy waters of the Mississippi. No sir, they were going home. He just needed to keep his senses and think of something. Looking around at the commotion, he saw men tearing off boards, posts, pieces of rail, anything that might keep a body afloat.

That was it. They needed something that would hold up two men until help could reach them. No sooner had he thought this, the answer came right at his feet. Two men close by had been fighting over a board, and as one of them pushed the other one over the rail, he too went over in the clutches of the first. Andrew sprang into action as he scooped up the plank that would save them.

"We're going over," Andrew shouted to Elijah. "Once we get to the lower deck, it'll be easier."

Andrew would have liked to have waited a little longer until the grappling swimmers were thinned out, but he was afraid someone would try to steal the board away. They could not survive without it. Andrew knew that Elijah wasn't strong enough to fight the current, but hopefully, he would be strong enough to lay across the board. So the two friends lifted the board, Elijah holding on to it with one hand and his crutch with the other, and headed for the plunge.

"I'll go first," Andrew shouted again. He looked at Elijah trying to hold on to the board. "Can you lift the board over to me?"

Elijah nodded.

Whether Elijah was strong enough or not, they had no choice. Andrew slipped over the rail and slid down a post to the deck below. There was even more madness here as men and women were in a frenzy to escape the fire, knocking each other into the water as they searched for safety.

There was no time to stop to watch or help. Andrew and Elijah had to get off the burning riverboat and away from the desperate crowd. As the board slid down from above, Andrew grasped it and looked around for anyone with a mind to take it from him. He was prepared to fight for the board, even if it meant knocking someone else in the water.

"Hurry, Elijah!" Andrew yelled up. He didn't know if his friend could hear him or not, but soon he saw the bandaged leg come over the rail. Just as Elijah landed on the lower deck, another loud, terrifying noise came from the center of the boat. The two friends looked up to see the huge wheelhouse break loose from the boat. As if in slow motion, the gigantic structure toppled in the water, taking with it all those who had been pitifully clinging to it. All went down into the depths of the cruel river.

To dwell on the horrible scene would be to paralyze your own movements for escape, so Andrew pushed on toward the edge of the deck. Much to his surprise, many of the people who had been thrashing in the water only minutes ago were gone. Some floated away with the current on anything they could get their hands on, live horses, dead mules, crates, and planks. Others had gone down into the dark waters never to be seen again.

"We're going in," Andrew stated solemnly. "It'll be all right."

Elijah looked at him with his sad, blue eyes. His former spirit of optimism had left him, leaving an empty shell of a man. But still he nodded in agreement.

Together they lowered the board near the water. Then with a big jump, Andrew and the board landed in the chilly river. Elijah followed quickly, and the two of them clung to the board as they drifted away from the blazing inferno. It was unbearable to hear the agonizing cries for help from those trapped by the flames. Even after all the horrors of the war, Andrew knew this would be the night that would haunt him for the rest of his life, if he survived that is.

After only a few minutes in the cold water, Andrew realized they could not endure it for very long. So he thought of a new plan. Spying a rope hanging down from the boat, he decided to swim to it and hold on there until the boat burned itself out. He called to Elijah to kick as hard as he could in the direction of the riverboat.

Slowly, they made their way back, and Andrew was able to grab the rope. Knowing Elijah didn't have the strength to hold onto the rope, Andrew used every ounce of strength he had to grip the board and the rope at the same time. And there, as his arms burned from the stress and his legs were numb from the cold, Andrew began to pray. He did not want to die here in this river. He wanted to see his Mary Louise, his family, and his home again. He wanted to live.

After what seemed like an eternity, the bright light of the flames turned into darkness. The cries and screams died away, and it was eerily silent. The mighty *Sultana* was gone, leaving only a charred hull. Andrew now looked up at the rope he had been clinging to and realized he did not have strength enough to pull himself up.

He called to Elijah, but there was no answer. In the dark Andrew couldn't see his friend at the other end of the board and called again.

"Elijah, wake up," he urged. "We have to get back on the hull."
Still no answer.

It was at that moment Andrew realized with shock and grief

that Elijah was not on the board. Andrew had no idea when his friend had given up and how long he had been on the board by himself. Andrew could not bear to think on it now. He would grieve for his friend forever, but now he had an even greater reason to save himself. Someone needed to tell their story, Elijah's story. They both could not disappear from this life without their loved ones knowing how they had struggled, what they had endured, and how they longed to be home.

And with that renewed spirit, Andrew let go of the board and clung to the rope with both hands. Somehow he had to find the strength to pull himself up.

Suddenly, the rope began to lift Andrew out of the water. Confused, he did not know what was happening, but he continued to cling to it with all his might. Soon he was being lifted by a pair of strong hands and pulled onto the hull. Looking up in the darkness, he saw the face of a young man. By the man's nightshirt and trousers, Andrew knew he was not an ex-prisoner but a passenger he had noticed before.

As Andrew lay in utter exhaustion unable to move, the young man began rubbing Andrew's numb legs to restore the circulation to them.

Remembering how insistent Elijah had been for Andrew to know the guard Thomas by name, how important he thought it was, Andrew needed to know the name of this person who had saved him.

Barely able to speak, Andrew whispered to the man, "What is your name?"

"Dee," he said as he worked vigorously to warm up Andrew's cold body.

Andrew simply nodded his head and closed his eyes. Barely audible, Andrew then added, "Thank you."

In a short time Andrew felt himself being lifted again and lowered onto a flat raft that was tied to a small wooden boat. There were other survivors on the raft and in the boat. Some were crying, others moaning, a few were more dead than alive. But all had been saved. Andrew had survived the disastrous night.

Before long, the loaded boat and raft pulled onto the shore, and its human cargo helped onto land and beside a warm fire. Soon a young boy who looked to be about twelve handed Andrew a cup of hot coffee.

Again Andrew asked, "What is your name, son?"

"I'm Joe, sir," he answered and moved on to serve another survivor.

Although the boy did not hear him, Andrew said, "Thank you."

11

Escape from the Blaze
April 27, 1865, 2:00 a.m.

A loud boom pierced the silence of the small, sleeping house. Joe sat up in bed, alarmed and half-asleep.

What was that? he thought.

Thunder, he told himself.

And with his groggy mind satisfied, he fell back on the pillow. Snuggling under his warm quilt, he drifted back into his dreams. He was having the most wonderful dream about the city, the people, and the excitement. In his dream he was not hiding under his hat or behind a barrel but right in the middle of the fun.

But then he heard voices; first his pa's, then Daniel's; soon he heard his ma's voice as well. Then Joe heard the sound of the front door opening and closing. He rose up on his elbows and listened. Something strange was going on in the rooms below his loft. He had no idea what his family could be doing in the middle of the night.

"Joe, wake up," called Pa. "Joe, get up son."

Something is definitely wrong, he thought now. *But what?*

Quickly, Joe jumped out of bed. He grabbed his pants from the chair and pulled them on, cramming his nightshirt inside as he buttoned them up.

"I'm up, Pa," Joe answered as he climbed down the ladder that led to his loft room. "I'm here, sir."

"Now listen, son," Pa began as he gathered his coat and put it on. "There's been an accident on the river. Looks like a boat has caught on fire. More'n likely it's that overcrowded one we saw today. Dang fools. Me and Daniel are taking the boat to see if we can help."

Pa stopped and took Joe by the shoulders, making sure he understood his instructions clearly.

"You get a fire going down on the bank, you hear?" Pa said squeezing his arms. "And help your ma fetch water to make some coffee. Can you do that?"

Joe had shaken his father's trust in him by leaving the boat to go on the day's adventure. Joe knew he would have to work hard to regain it, and this was a good starting point.

"Yes sir," Joe said with determination in his voice. He would show Pa he could handle the responsibility.

Quickly, Daniel and Pa gathered some rope and a few blankets and were out the door into the darkness. It wasn't until Joe stepped outside to build the fire that he saw the terrible blaze in the distance to the north. That's when the reality of the situation set in. If the riverboat was the *Sultana*, then it meant that Elizabeth and her family were there now in dreadful danger. He could not imagine what they must be going through right at this moment. All kinds of terrible thoughts were running through his mind, and the only way to stop it was to keep himself busy with his task.

As he gathered wood for the fire, Joe could hear noises from the direction of the boat, more loud crashes, and, no, it couldn't be possible, but, yes, he thought he heard the cries of people. It was more than he could bear. He wished with all his heart that he could have gone with Pa and Daniel to help rescue those people. But he did his job and had a fire blazing up in a few minutes as he kept his eye on the bigger blaze on the river. Then he went to the well and dropped the bucket into the darkness, pulling it right back up, heavy now with water. As the contents sloshed on his pants, he carried the bucket inside to his ma. She was busy putting a large pan of biscuits in the oven. The sight gave him hope that Pa would be able to save lots of people from the terrible waters of the Mississippi.

Joe wasted no time in replacing the bucket at the well and

getting back to keep the fire going. Pa and Daniel should be returning soon, and his fire had to be good and hot. Searching for more wood, Joe tried to keep his eyes off the flames of the giant riverboat now. Watching was too painful and even more painful was thinking about what was happening to the people on her. He wished Pa and Daniel would hurry and get back.

In just a few minutes his wish was granted. Hearing the boat scrape the ground as it pulled onto shore, Joe ran to help Pa and Daniel unload the passengers. They had picked up about ten men, all soaked and shivering from the cold. Some were fully dressed, but others had shed all their clothes in an attempt to swim better. Most of them could barely walk. All were exhausted, falling out on the ground beside the warm fire.

Ma and Joe began their rounds of passing out cups of hot coffee and warm biscuits. Some of the men were bleeding from bad gashes in their heads, arms, or legs, and Ma got busy cleaning and bandaging their wounds. Somehow, she had time to put another pan of biscuits in the oven and have more coffee ready when Pa and Daniel came in with the next group.

Sometime in all Joe's efforts to keep the fire going strong and pass out the cups of coffee, he looked up to see darkness where the blazing riverboat had been. The magnificent *Sultana* had burned down to her hull, and this made his heart sink. Worry over what had happened to Elizabeth and her family was making him sick. It was a good thing he was so busy, or he might just break down and cry like a baby.

As Joe continued to feed the fire and tend to the survivors, he realized these men were no longer numb with cold but numb from shock as they sat dazed and confused with glazed-over eyes. All but one, that is. With clear eyes, a soldier who had asked Joe his name had been watching Joe's every move and looking around at the others with the saddest, most distressed look on his face. Wanting to help somehow, Joe spoke to him.

"Can I do something for you, sir?" asked Joe.

The young man just continued to stare at him, as if he hadn't heard. Then he shook his head and mumbled, "Can't nothing be done now. I lost him, that's it. I lost him."

Confused, Joe said, "Lost who?"

Andrew looked at Joe as if it were a really dumb question.

"Elijah," he answered. "Elijah, of course. I was supposed to save him. We're going home, you know. We're going home together."

Andrew shook his head over and over again.

"But he's gone," Andrew rubbed his face with both his hands. "He's gone for good . . . and nothing can be done now. It's too late, too late."

Joe wanted to comfort this poor, hurting man, but he didn't

know what to do. If the young soldier would break down in tears, Joe might put his hand on the man's shoulder. But, oddly, he didn't shed a tear. He simply stared at Joe in the most disturbing way.

Just then, Pa and Daniel returned with another boatload of rescued passengers, and Joe was relieved to have the distraction to keep him busy.

"This here's the last of the men on the hull," Pa grunted as he carried an injured man across his shoulder. "Just in time, too. The thing nearly capsized us as it went down."

Joe helped Pa lay the man near the fire.

"That there's the man who did it," Pa was pointing to a figure coming out of the darkness toward the fire. "He put every last one of these fellows into our boat. Barely made it off himself."

As Joe watched, the hero moved closer and looked up. Joe's heart leaped with joy.

It was the girl's brother. It was Dee.

12

Approaching Dawn
April 27, 1865

As the dark sky lightened up and the stars began to fade away, Pa and Daniel made one last search in the water. They had seen rescue boats beginning to move about and knew that the people in town and on the docked boats had been alerted. Soon Pa and Daniel would be needed to help load the survivors in their own yard for the journey to the opposite shore and a good doctor. With a tired body and aching arms, Joe helped shove the boat into the water for the last time.

In an hour, daylight would come and with it, a welcome relief for the many pitiful souls who had been clinging to anything that would keep them out of the current. The flooded river had covered the shoreline, leaving only the tops of trees visible, and here men were holding on with their last ounce of strength. Rescue could not come soon enough for them. Sadly, it would come too late for many.

As Joe watched his pa and Daniel move away from the bank, he thought about the lively girl who had pulled him away from his boat and into her adventure. Surely her brother would know what had happened to her, but Joe had not gotten the nerve to approach him and ask. Dee had such a sad, far-away look on his face that Joe did not want to disturb him. Not wanting to admit it, Joe was also afraid to hear the answer. He wanted to stay hopeful and believe she was wrapped in a blanket on a rescue boat somewhere.

Just then, Joe heard his ma call him. He ran for the house just in time to help her carry a bucket of water inside. As tired as she was, Ma continued to boil water for coffee and put biscuits in the oven. Joe tried to help as much as possible. Wet from carrying the water bucket and cold from the night air, Joe lingered in the house by his own fire. He wished he could just stay there until all the survivors were taken away. He could no longer bear to hear the moans and cries of those who had been badly burned, or look on the ghostly stares of those in shock. His heart was breaking for the ones who were crying over the loss of their friends. As he sat warming himself, Joe knew he had to find the strength to go back outside.

When the biscuits were done, Joe took the hot pan from his ma, wrapped it in a heavy cloth, and headed out the door.

As soon as Joe neared the fire, he knew something was wrong. In the pre-dawn light, it was impossible to see what was going on. Pa and Daniel had returned and were putting bundles of something on the ground. He could see a man on his knees beside the fire.

What is that sound? Joe asked himself as he was drawn to the scene.

Suddenly he knew what the sound was. It was weeping, loud, agonizing weeping. Joe had never heard such a heartbreaking cry, and he inched closer to see what was going on. When he got close enough to see, he dropped the whole pan of biscuits and fell on his knees as well.

Lying there on the cold ground was the beautiful, young girl named Elizabeth. She looked as if she were in a peaceful, deep sleep. Her face was smooth but pale. Her lips were blue, yet she was still lovely. Joe expected her to sit up and smile at him, anxious to go on a new adventure. He wanted her to pull on his shirt and drag him away as she had done only a few hours ago. He wanted her to push him into Pa's boat and order him to take her across to the city. He wanted her to live out her dreams and marry the man whom she believed was waiting on her. But she was as still as stone and in the sleep from which you never wake.

Joe's mind could hardly conceive of what was happening. Not

only was the body of Elizabeth by the fire, but a young girl was also there beside her. She must be the younger sister Elizabeth had mentioned.

How can this be happening? thought Joe. *Oh, please, not these beautiful, young girls. Not them. No, no, not both of them.*

Joe hid his face in his hands and let all the pent-up emotions come pouring out. There on the cold ground, he cried for the two girls lying lifeless on the ground. He cried for the many people who had died, and their families who would never see them again. He cried for the survivors who would never be the same after this night, and he cried because he was completely exhausted and couldn't do anything else.

A few feet away Dee was sitting on the ground between his two sisters, moving from one to the other as he cried. First rocking Catherine as he held her then laying his body across Elizabeth, he cried more like an animal than a human. As he sobbed, he was saying over and over, "I should have saved them," he wailed. "No, no, no. I should have saved them."

Finally Pa could stand it no longer and kneeled down to comfort Dee.

"Please, son, please," Pa pleaded as he touched Dee's shoulder. "Look at all these lives you saved. You did all you could."

"No, no, no," was all Dee could say between his sobs.

Seeing that his words were doing nothing to ease the young man's pain, Pa rose and went to the boat to get an oilcloth to cover the two bodies.

That's when Joe snapped out of his crying and jumped into action.

"Wait, Pa," he called. "Wait one minute."

Then Joe ran back to the house, burst in the door, and climbed up the ladder to his loft. He grabbed the quilt from off his bed, the one his grandma had made for him, and descended the ladder.

Slowing down as he approached Dee, Joe held out the quilt. "Here, sir, use this," Joe laid the quilt beside Dee.

Paralyzed from his grief, Dee paid no attention to Joe or the quilt. He continued to hold Catherine, stroking her hair, and to lean over Elizabeth's body, touching her face. He would not allow anyone to come close.

Not knowing what to do, Joe just stood there. His tears made narrow streaks down his dirty face as he watched. Finally, Joe felt a hand touch his shoulder, and he looked back.

"Here, son, let me have it," Andrew whispered in a soft voice.

Joe stared at the soldier who had lost his dearest friend and didn't shed a single tear. Yet now the man's eyes were full and, like Joe, they made tiny streaks down his sooty face. His hands were shaking as he reached out.

Finding it too difficult to speak, Joe handed Andrew the quilt without a word. Andrew then knelt down beside Dee and began talking to him. Joe couldn't hear what he was saying to Dee, but whatever it was, the words were powerful enough. In only a few minutes, Dee and Andrew stood up. They each took a corner of Joe's quilt and laid it over the two girls. This simple act of protecting and comforting his sisters in this way helped Dee to calm down. As the eastern sky began to turn pink, the three strangers who now shared a common grief sat on the ground together and watched the sun rise.

The new day brought relief for the weary survivors who waited to be rescued. But it also brought to light the reality of the horrible events that had happened in the darkness. So many lives were lost. So many lives were changed forever, and the remains of the magnificent *Sultana* now lay at the bottom of the Mississippi.

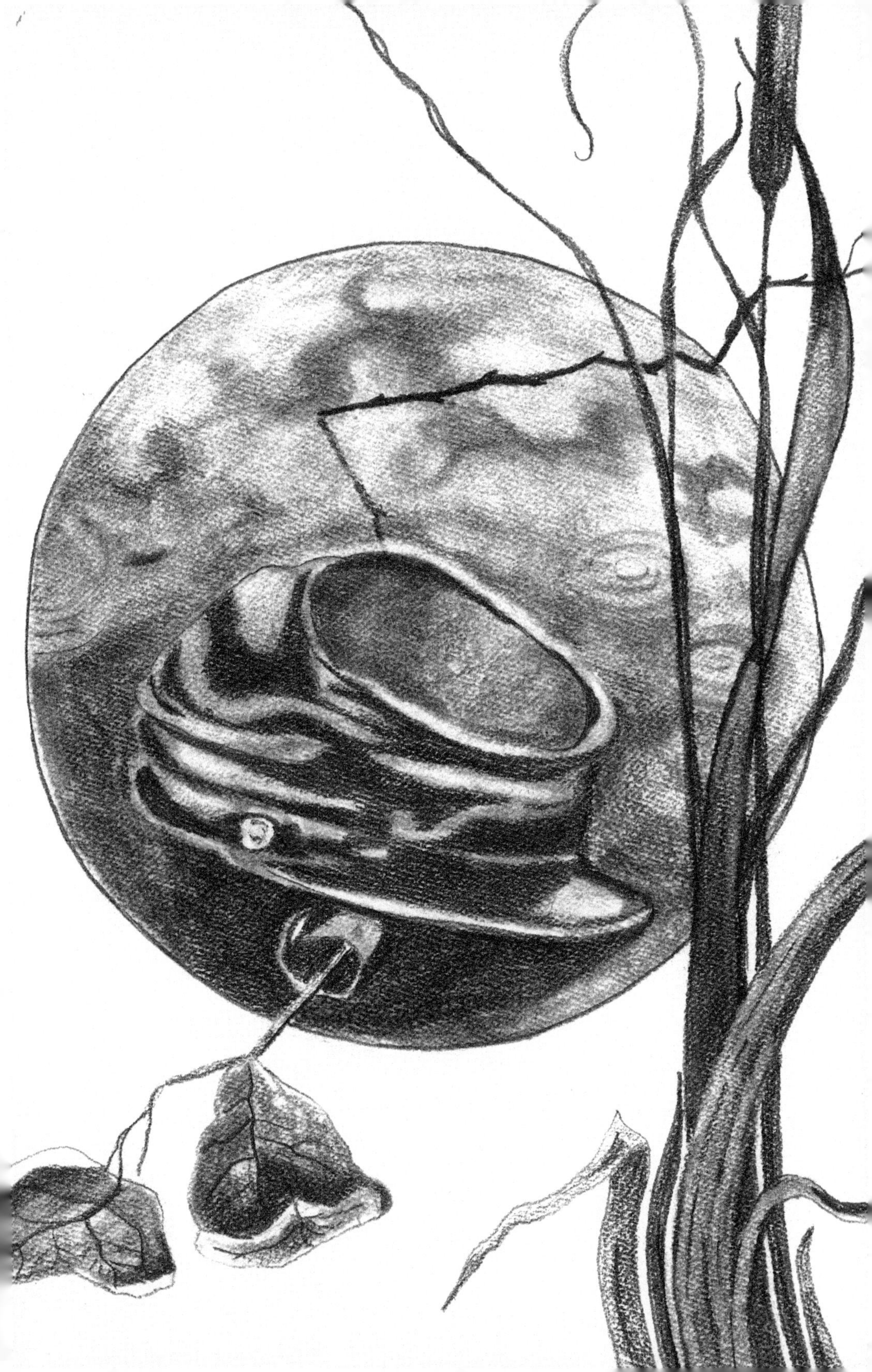

The Aftermath
April 27, 1865

In the blink of an eye, it seemed, Dee lost everything. Although he spent weeks in Memphis searching the hospitals, riding up and down the river, and posting notices about his parents, he never found them. He had no money, no home, nothing by which to remember his past life, and no hopes for the future. With the charity of the people of Memphis, he buried his sisters and marked their graves with a headstone. Despite his fear, Dee would eventually board another riverboat to complete his family's journey. Alone.

His life would be forever filled with nightmares of that disastrous night, and his heart would never stop grieving for his high-spirited sister Elizabeth. One life snuffed out too early, the other life changed forever.

Once again, the young soldier Andrew had survived when so

many others had perished. Though he never understood why he was spared, he lived out a life full of nightmares, memories, and grief. For weeks he would walk the streets of Memphis, check the hospitals, and talk with the crewmen of boats on the river. Refusing to give up hope, he continued to search for Elijah. Andrew felt he could not go home without his dearest friend.

Finally, after weeks of searching, it became too exhausting for Andrew, and with a heavy heart and fearful soul, he boarded another riverboat going north. Leaving without his friend was unbearable. The thought of Elijah's body being at the bottom of the cold Mississippi or lodged somewhere along its banks was more than he could endure. But his heart yearned to be home. He ached to see Mary Louise and ask for her hand in marriage. He needed to begin living his life.

Some years later, Andrew finally understood his purpose for surviving the battles, the hardships of prison, and the terrible disaster. Holding his newborn, he named the boy Elijah. Andrew would tell his little son all about his close friend and their time together. In this little child, this new life, his friend would live on.

After a few days Joe and his family stopped talking about the terrible night. But none of them would ever forget it. Every time Joe walked along the bank by the river, he would look toward the north and spy a tall rod extending from the water. It was all that was left of the magnificent *Sultana.* The sight always stung his eyes and his heart, and he would find himself choking back tears.

When Pa and Daniel went to Memphis for supplies, Joe made excuses not to go. Pa understood and didn't press his son. Pa knew that the horrific night had affected Joe more than the rest of the family, and Joe should not be pushed to get on the river. The way Joe had reacted to the young girl who had died in the blast made Pa suspect there was some connection between her and the day Joe went to Main Street. One day he would ask Joe to tell the whole story of that day.

Although Joe would live on the banks of the Mississippi for the rest of his life, he would always fear it. When he grew to be a young man and married, he built a home for his new wife right along the bank of the river near his family's home. Within the year his wife bore him a beautiful baby girl. Joe named her Elizabeth.

THE END

THE CHARACTERS

Based on true events and people, historical fiction brings the past into a real-life setting. The characters in this story are based on real people who were involved in the disaster of the *Sultana*. The brave young brother Dee was created from a young man named DeWitt Clinton Spikes. He was the lone survivor of eight members of his immediate family and four other relatives. He is credited with saving the lives of thirty men from the burned-out riverboat.

Elizabeth is drawn from one of the Spikes's daughters. Susan Spikes was seventeen years old at the time of her death. She and her mother Esther are buried at Elmwood Cemetery in Memphis. There was a younger sister in the family, her name unknown, from which the character Catherine was created.

The ex-prisoner-of-war Andrew portrays a real Union soldier named Andrew Peery. He was captured at the fort at Sulphur Branch Trestle in Alabama and imprisoned at Cahaba. Rescued from the *Sultana*, he was taken to the Arkansas shore and laid beside a fire. Later he was transported to Memphis and eventually made it to his home in the north. Although his friend Elijah could have existed, this character is completely fictional. His story represents many of the unfortunate soldiers aboard the ill-fated *Sultana*.

The young boy Joe comes from a family named Fogelman. John Fogelman and his two sons, Dallas and Leroy, rescued stranded men from the burning bow of the *Sultana* with their raft and delivered them to the Arkansas side of the river. Although the real sons were both older than twelve, a younger Joe seemed to fit the story better.

Whether or not any of these characters ever met is doubtful, maybe impossible, but they all shared the same experience when the giant riverboat exploded. This is the story of only a few of the lost and the saved. There are thousands of other stories that will forever remain untold.

THE *SULTANA*

In the mid-1800s riverboats were the *Queens* of the Mississippi River. Both elegant and powerful they steamed up and down the great waters carrying passengers and cargo. The *Sultana* appeared on the river in 1863, one of the largest riverboats of her time. Having four boilers and water wheels on each of her sides, she could push through the current without much drag. Her capacity was approximately 376 passengers, but on the night of the explosion, she was carrying at least 2,300 passengers and possibly as many as 2,500.

The cause of the explosion that ripped through the middle of the giant riverboat was never positively established. There was much debate over the issue. Some think it was the weak patch job done on the boiler in Vicksburg. Others think it was the weight of the overload of passengers causing the boilers to overheat and explode. One theory pointed to a flaw in the design of the boiler itself that caused a build-up of sediment, which in turn, caused it to become overheated. A few believe it was the result of sabotage, a torpedo planted in the fuel that was shoveled into the boiler. This is truly past history, and the evidence that could settle the matter has been virtually erased. The true cause of the disaster may never be known.

ABOUT THE AUTHOR

For thirty-four years Nancy has been teaching children to read. During this time she has read thousands of stories with her students and grandchildren. Combining this love for reading and her love for writing she began writing stories about the past for young readers. Her hope is that children will learn about history and life's challenges through enjoyable stories.

Nancy lives in Memphis, Tennessee with her husband, Earl. She enjoys spending time with her two daughters and four grandchildren. She has a Bachelor's degree from Arkansas State University and a Master's degree in Education from University of Memphis. She currently teaches at Presbyterian Day School.

OTHER BOOKS BY NANCY GENTRY

www.RebelInPetticoats.com